CHILDREN'S THRIFT CLASSICS

The War of the Worlds

H. G. WELLS

Adapted by Bob Blaisdell
Illustrated by John Green

DOVER PUBLICATIONS, INC.
Mineola, New York

DOVER CHILDREN'S THRIFT CLASSICS

EDITOR OF THIS VOLUME: SUSAN L. RATTINER

Copyright

Bibliographical Note

This Dover edition, first published in 1999, is a new abridgment of *The War of the Worlds,* originally published by William Heinemann, London, in 1898. The illustrations have been specially prepared for this edition.

Library of Congress Cataloging-in-Publication Data

Wells, H. G. (Herbert George), 1866–1946.
The war of the worlds / H.G. Wells ; adapted by Bob Blaisdell ; illustrated by John Green.
p. cm. — (Dover children's thrift classics)
"This Dover edition . . . is a new abridgment . . . originally published by William Heinemann, London, in 1898. The illustrations have been specially prepared for this edition"—T.p. verso.
Summary: As life on Mars becomes impossible, Martians and their terrifying machines invade the earth.
ISBN 0-486-40552-4 (pbk.)
[1. Science fiction.] I. Blaisdell, Robert. II. Green, John, 1948– ill. III. Title. IV. Series.
PZ7.W4647War 1999
[Fic]—DC21 99-11174
CIP

Manufactured in the United States of America
Dover Publications, Inc., 31 East 2nd Street, Mineola, N.Y. 11501

Contents

Looking through the telescope at Mars, I saw three faint points of light.

1. The Falling Star

IN THE LAST years of the nineteenth century no one would have believed that this world was being watched by mortal creatures more intelligent than man. As we busied ourselves about our various concerns we were being watched and studied, perhaps in just the way we, with a microscope, might study the miniature life-forms in a drop of water. No one gave a thought to the older worlds of space as sources of human danger. At most, we fancied there might be other men upon Mars, perhaps less developed than we. Yet across that gulf of space, minds that are to our minds as ours are to those of our dogs regarded this earth and slowly and surely drew their plans against us.

The planet Mars revolves around the sun at a distance of 140,000,000 miles, and the light and heat it receives from the sun is barely half of that received by this world. It must be older than our world, and long before Earth reached a temperature that would allow any life to exist, life upon Mars must have begun.

The cooling that must someday overtake our planet has already gone far with our neighbor. Even in its warmest areas, its midday temperature barely approaches that of our coldest winter. Its oceans have shrunk until they cover but a third of its surface. The immediate pressure of finding ways to live has sharpened the Martians' minds and hardened their hearts. And looking across space with instruments such as we have scarcely dreamed of, they see, at its nearest distance of only 35,000,000 miles, our own warmer planet, green with vegetation and blue with water, with a cloudy atmosphere.

We men, the creatures who inhabit Earth, must be to Martians at least as strange and lowly as are the monkeys to us. Our world is crowded with life, but crowded with what they regard as inferior animals. To move closer to the sun is, indeed, their only escape from the destruction that creeps upon them.

Before we judge of them too harshly we must remember what ruthless and utter destruction our own species has brought to animals and our own fellow men. The Tasmanians were almost entirely swept out of existence by European immigrants. Are we to complain if the Martians dealt with us in the same way?

Six years ago now the astronomer Lavelle noticed through his telescope a huge outbreak of gas upon Mars. He followed up with his spectroscope and saw an indication of a mass of flaming gas moving very quickly towards this earth. Lavelle compared it to a colossal puff of flame suddenly and violently squirted out of the planet.

Yet the next day there was nothing of this in the papers except a little note in the *Daily Telegraph,* and the world went on ignorant of one of the gravest dangers that ever threatened the human race. I might not have heard of the Martian eruption at all had I not met Ogilvy, the well-known astronomer. He was immensely excited at the news, and invited me up to take a turn with him that night in watching the red planet.

Looking through his telescope at Mars, one saw a circle of deep blue and the little round planet swimming in space. It seemed such a little thing, faintly marked with stripes, and slightly flattened from the perfect round. It was forty million miles from us. But near Mars were three faint points of light. Invisible to me, however, because it was so remote and small, flying swiftly and steadily towards me across that incredible distance, drawing nearer every minute by so many thousands of miles, came the Thing they were sending us, the Thing that was to bring so much struggle and calamity and death to the earth. I never dreamed of it then as I watched; no one on Earth dreamed of it.

That night, too, there was another jetting out of gas from the distant planet. I saw it. A reddish flash on the edge, just as the clock struck midnight; I told Ogilvy and he took my place behind the telescope. He exclaimed, "Oh!" at the streamer of gas that came out from Mars.

That night another invisible missile started on its way to Earth, twenty-four hours after the first one.

Ogilvy was full of ideas that night about what we had seen. He scoffed at the idea of Mars having inhabitants who were signalling to us. He thought that meteorites might be falling in a heavy shower upon the planet, or that a huge volcanic explosion was taking place. "The chances against anything manlike on Mars are a million to one," he said.

Hundreds of observers saw the flame that night and the night after about midnight, and again the night after; and so for ten nights, a flame each night. Even the daily papers woke up to the disturbances, and articles appeared here and there about volcanoes upon Mars.

It seems to me now almost wonderful that, with fate hanging over us, men could go about their petty concerns as they did. For my own part, I was busy learning to ride a bicycle, and writing a series of essays about the development of mankind's moral ideas.

One night (the first missile then could scarcely have been 10,000,000 miles away), I went for a walk with my wife. It was starlight, and I explained the signs of the zodiac to her, and pointed out Mars, a bright dot of light, towards which so many telescopes were pointed. The warm night seemed so safe and tranquil.

Then came the night of the first falling star. It was seen early in the morning, rushing eastward, a line of flame high in the atmosphere. Hundreds must have seen it, and taken it for an ordinary falling star.

I was at home at that hour and writing in my study; and although my windows faced that direction, I saw nothing of it. Yet this strangest of all things that ever came to Earth from outer space must have fallen while I was sitting there, visible to me had I only looked up as it passed. Some of those who saw its flight say it travelled with a hissing sound. Many people in Berkshire, Surrey, and Middlesex must have seen the fall of it, but no one seems to have troubled to look for the fallen "meteorite" that night.

But very early in the morning poor Ogilvy, who had seen the shooting star and who was persuaded that a meteorite lay somewhere on the common between Horsell, Ottershaw, and Woking, rose early with the idea of finding it. Find it he did, soon after dawn, and not far from the sandpits. An enormous hole had been made by the impact of the object, and the sand and gravel had been flung in every direction over the heath, forming heaps visible a mile and a half away. The heather was on fire eastward, and a thin blue smoke rose against the dawn.

The Thing itself lay almost entirely buried in sand, amidst the scattered splinters of a fir tree it had shivered to fragments in its landing. The uncovered part of it had the appearance of a huge cylinder, caked over and its outline softened by a thick, scaly crust. It had a diameter of about thirty yards. He approached the mass, surprised at the size and more so at the shape, since most meteorites are round. It was, however, still so hot from its flight through the air as to forbid his near approach. He heard a stirring noise within the cylinder, which he believed to be the unequal cooling between the center and the surface. It did not occur to him that it might be hollow.

He remained standing at the edge of the pit that the Thing had made for itself, staring at the strange appearance, astonished chiefly at its unusual shape and color. The early morning was strangely still, and the sun, just clearing the pine trees, was already warm. He did not remember hearing any birds that morning, there was certainly no breeze stirring, and the only sounds were the faint movements from within the cylinder. He was all alone on the common.

Then suddenly he noticed that some of the grayish crust that covered the meteorite was falling off the circular edge of the end. It was dropping off in flakes and raining down upon the sand. A large piece suddenly fell off and fell with a sharp noise.

Although the heat was almost overpowering, Ogilvy decided he had to investigate, and clambered down into the pit close to the bulk to see the Thing more clearly. Then he noticed that, very slowly, the circular top of the cylinder was rotating on its body. He heard a muffled grating sound and saw the top jerk forward an inch or so. The cylinder was hollow—with an end that screwed out! Something within the cylinder was unscrewing the top!

"Good heavens!" said Ogilvy. "There's a man in it—or several men in it! Half roasted to death! Trying to escape!"

At once, with a quick mental leap, he linked the Thing with the flash upon Mars.

The thought of the poor creature within so troubled him that for a moment he forgot the heat and went forward to the cylinder to help turn the top. But luckily the intensity of the heat stopped him before he could burn his hands on the still-glowing metal. At that he decided to go for help, and scrambled out the pit, running off toward Woking. It must have been somewhere around six o'clock. He met a waggoner and tried to make him understand, but the tale he told and his appearance were so wild that the man simply drove on. He was equally unsuccessful with the man who was just unlocking the doors of the pub near Horsell Bridge. The fellow thought Ogilvy was a lunatic. When he saw Henderson, the London newspaperman, in his garden, he called over the fence and said, "You saw that shooting star last night?"

"What of it?" said Henderson.

"It's out on Horsell Common now."

"Good Lord!" said Henderson. "A fallen meteorite! That's a good story."

"But it's something more than a meteorite. It's a cylinder—there's something inside."

"What are you saying, Ogilvy?"

Ogilvy told him all that he had seen. Henderson dropped his spade, snatched up his jacket and came out into the road. The two men hurried back at once to the common, and found the cylinder still lying in the same position. But now the sounds inside had stopped, and a thin circle of bright metal showed between the top and the body of the cylinder. Air was either entering or escaping at the rim with a thin, sizzling sound.

They listened, rapped on the scaly burnt metal with a stick, and, meeting with no response, they both concluded the man or men inside must have passed out or be dead.

They went off back to the town to get help. One can imagine them, covered with sand, excited and confused, running up the little street in the bright sunlight just as the shop folks were taking down their shutters and people were opening their bedroom windows. Henderson went into the railway station at once to telegraph the news to London.

By eight o'clock a number of boys and unemployed men had already started for the common to see the "dead men from Mars." That was the form the story had taken. I heard of it first from my newspaper boy around a quarter to nine. I was naturally startled, and lost no time in going out and across the Ottershaw bridge to the sand pits.

I found a little crowd of perhaps twenty people surrounding the huge hole into which the cylinder lay. There were four or five boys sitting on the edge of the pit, with their feet dangling, and amusing themselves—until I stopped them—by throwing stones at the giant metal mass.

Most of the people there were staring quietly at the end of the cylinder, which was as still as Ogilvy and Henderson had left it. I believe the crowd was disappointed not to see a heap of charred bodies. Some went away while I was there, and others came. I clambered into the pit and fancied I heard a faint movement under my feet.

It was only when I got this close to it that the strangeness of this object was at all evident to me. At the first glance it was really no more exciting than an overturned carriage or a tree blown over across the road. It required a certain amount of scientific education to perceive that the scales on the gray metal were unusual and that the yellowish-white metal that gleamed in the crack between the lid and the cylinder had an unfamiliar color.

At that time it was quite clear in my own mind that the Thing had come from the planet Mars, but I doubted it could contain a living creature. I thought the unscrewing of the lid might be automatic. I wondered what objects could be inside. But nothing seemed to be happening, so, about eleven, I walked back home to Maybury.

In the afternoon the appearance of the common had changed. The early editions of the evening newspapers had startled London with enormous headlines:

A MESSAGE RECEIVED FROM MARS

REMARKABLE STORY FROM WOKING

There were half a dozen carriages or more from the Woking station standing in the road by the sandpits. Besides that, there was quite a heap of bicycles. In addition, a large number of people must have walked, in spite of the heat of the day, from Woking and Chertsey, so that there was altogether quite a considerable crowd—one or two fancily dressed ladies among them.

It was glaringly hot, not a cloud in the sky nor a breath of wind, and the only shadow was that of the few scattered pine trees. The heather that had been on fire had been put out, but the level ground towards Ottershaw was blackened as far as one could see.

Going to the edge of the pit, I found it occupied by a

group of about half a dozen men—Henderson, Ogilvy, and a tall, fair-haired man that I afterwards learned was Stent, the Royal Astronomer, with several workmen digging away with spades and pickaxes. Stent was giving directions and standing atop the cylinder, which was now evidently cool enough.

A large portion of the cylinder had been uncovered, though its lower end was still buried. As soon as Ogilvy saw me among the staring crowd at the edge of the pit he called to me to come down, and asked me if I would mind going over to see Lord Hilton, the lord of the manor.

The growing crowd, he said, was making their digging much harder than necessary, especially the boys. They wanted a light railing put up, and help to keep the people back. He told me that a faint stirring was still coming from within the cylinder, but that the workmen had been unable to unscrew the top, as they could get no grip on it. The casing appeared to be enormously thick, and it was possible that the faint sounds came from deep within.

I was very glad to do as he asked, and so become one of the privileged spectators within the hoped-for enclosure. I failed to find Lord Hilton at his house, but I was told he was expected from London by the six o'clock train from Waterloo; and as it was then about a quarter past five, I went home, had some tea, and walked up to the station to find him.

2. The Cylinder Opens

WHEN I returned to the common the sun was setting. Scattered groups were hurrying from the direction of Woking, and one or two persons were returning. The crowd about the pit had increased and stood out black against the lemon-yellow of the sky—a couple of hundred people, perhaps. There were raised voices, and some sort of struggle appeared to be going on about the pit. As I drew nearer I heard Stent saying: "Keep back! Keep back!"

A neighbor child named Max came running towards me.

"It's a movin'," he said to me as he passed. "It's a-screwin', and a-screwin' out. I don't like it. I'm a-goin' 'ome, I am."

I went on. The crowd was elbowing and jostling one another.

"He's fallen into the pit!" cried someone.

"Keep back!" cried others.

I elbowed my way through, and I heard a peculiar humming sound from the pit.

"I say!" said Ogilvy, seeing me, "help keep these idiots back. We don't know what's in the confounded thing, you know!"

I saw a young man standing on the cylinder and trying to scramble out of the hole again. The crowd had pushed him in.

The end of the cylinder was being screwed out from within. Nearly two feet of shining screw showed. Somebody pushed against me, and I narrowly missed falling onto the top of the screw. I looked behind me, and as I did so the screw must have come out, for the lid of the cylinder fell upon the gravel with a ringing thud. I turned my head towards the Thing again. I had the sunset in my eyes, and for a moment that circular hole on top seemed perfectly black.

I think everyone expected to see a man emerge—possibly something a little unlike us men, but in all essentials a man. I know I did. But, looking, I now saw something stirring within the shadow: grayish, floating movements, one above the other, then two bright circles—like eyes. Then something resembling a little gray snake, about the thickness of a walking stick, coiled up out of the writhing middle and wriggled in the air towards me—and then another snaky thing.

There was a loud shriek from a woman. I half-turned, keeping my eyes fixed upon the cylinder, from which other tentacles were now coming out. I saw surprise giving way to horror on the faces of the people around me. I heard groans and shouts. There was a general movement backward by the crowd. I, however, stood petrified and staring.

A big gray round bulk, the size, perhaps, of a bear, was rising slowly and painfully out of the cylinder. As it bulged up and caught the light, it glistened like wet leather.

Two large dark-colored eyes were watching me. The mass that framed the eyes, the head of the thing, was rounded, and had a face. There was a mouth under the eyes, the lipless edge of which quivered and panted, and drooled saliva. A long tentacle gripped the edge of the cylinder and another swayed in the air.

Those who have never seen a living Martian can scarcely imagine the strange horror of its appearance. The peculiar V-shaped mouth with its pointed upper lip, the absence of brow ridges, the absence of a chin beneath the wedgelike lower lip, the quivering of the mouth, the snaky groups of tentacles, the heavy breathing of the

I stood petrified as a big gray round bulk rose slowly out of the cylinder.

lungs in this strange atmosphere, the evident heaviness and painfulness of movement due to the greater pull of gravity of the Earth and the huge weird eyes—intense and monstrous. There was something spongy about the oily brown skin, something in the slow, awkward movements unspeakably nasty. Even at this first sight, I was overcome with disgust and dread.

Suddenly the monster vanished. It had toppled over the brim of the cylinder and fallen into the pit, with a thud like the fall of a great mass of wet leather. I heard it give a strange thick cry, and then another of these creatures appeared in the deep shadow of the opening.

I turned and, running madly, made for the first group of trees, perhaps a hundred yards away. There, among some pine trees, I stopped, panting, and waited further developments. The common around the sandpits was dotted with people, standing like myself in a half-fascinated terror, staring at these creatures, or rather at the heaped gravel at the edge of the pit in which they lay. And then, with a renewed horror, I saw a round, black object bobbing up and down at the edge of the pit. It was the head of the shopman who had fallen in, but showing as a little black object against the hot western sky. Now he got his shoulder and knee up, and again he seemed to slip back until only his head was visible. Suddenly he vanished, and I heard a faint shriek. I wanted to make myself go back and help him, but my fears stopped me.

Everything was then quite invisible, hidden by the deep pit and the heap of sand that the fall of the cylinder had made. There were still more than a hundred of us standing in a wide circle, in ditches, behind bushes, behind gates and hedges, saying little to one another and staring hard at a few heaps of sand.

I did not dare go back towards the pit, but I so wanted to peer into it. I began walking, therefore, in a big curve, seeking some vantage point. Suddenly a clump of thin black whips, like the arms of an octopus, flashed out of the pit and then withdrew, and afterwards a thin rod rose up, at the top of which spun a disk. What was this?

The sunset faded to twilight before anything further happened. As the dusk came on, more people began to arrive from Woking, and because of the stillness from the pit, we began to slowly advance towards it again. And then, within thirty yards of the pit, advancing from the direction of Horsell, I noted a little group of men, the first of whom was waving a white flag. These were the representatives from Horsell. It had been decided to show the Martians that we were intelligent creatures.

Flutter, flutter, went the flag. It was too far and too dark for me to recognize anyone there, but afterwards I learned that Ogilvy, Stent, and Henderson were among the group. A number of people followed the group at a little distance.

Suddenly there was a flash of light, and large puffs of greenish smoke came out of the pit, straight up into the air. This flame-like smoke was so bright that the deep blue sky overhead lit up for a moment. At the same time a faint hissing sound came from the pit.

Beyond the pit stood the little clot of people with the white flag. As the green smoke arose, their faces flashed out green, and faded again as the smoke vanished. Then slowly the hissing turned into a humming, and then into a long, loud drone. Slowly a humped shade rose out of the pit, and a beam of light flickered out from it.

Flashes of fire leapt from one man to another. It was as if each man were suddenly turned into a column of fire.

Then, by the flames by which they burned, I saw them staggering and falling, and their followers turning to run.

I stood staring, not yet realizing that this was Death leaping from man to man in that crowd. All I felt was that it was something very strange. An almost noiseless and blinding flash of light, and a man fell headlong and lay still; and as the unseen spear of fire passed over them, pine trees burst into flame. And far away towards Knaphill I saw the flashes of trees and hedges and wooden buildings suddenly set alight.

It was sweeping round swiftly and steadily, this flaming death, this invisible sword of heat. I saw it coming towards me by the flashing bushes it touched, and was too surprised to move. I heard the crackle of fire in the sand pits and the sudden squeal of a horse. Then the hissing and humming stopped, and the black, domelike object sank slowly out of sight into the pit.

All this had happened with such swiftness that I had stood motionless, dumbfounded and dazzled by the flashes of light. Had that death-ray swept full circle, I would have been killed.

The common now seemed almost black, except where its roadways lay gray and pale under the deep blue sky of the early night. Overhead the stars were coming out, and in the west the sky was still a pale, bright blue. The Martians and their tools of destruction were out of sight. Patches of bushes and trees were still smoking, and the houses towards Woking were sending up spires of flame into the night.

The little group of men with the white flag had been swept out of existence, and yet the evening was quiet and still. It came to me that I was upon this dark common, helpless, unprotected, and alone. I turned and began a stumbling run through the heather.

Once I had turned I did not dare to look back. I felt as if the Martians were playing with me, and that when I was upon the verge of safety their death-ray would leap after me from the pit and strike me down.

I remember nothing of my escape except the blundering against trees and stumbling through the heather. I came into the road between the crossroads and Horsell, and ran along this to the crossroads.

At last I could go no further. I was exhausted, and I staggered and tumbled by the side of the road near the bridge. I fell asleep, and when I awoke, I rose and walked unsteadily up to the bridge. It was still night, and I passed over the bridge.

I stopped at a group of people, two men and a woman, gathered by one of the houses.

"What news from the common?" said I.

"Eh?" said one of the men. "Ain't yer just been there?"

"People seem fair silly about the common," said the woman. "What's it all about?"

"Haven't you heard of the men from Mars?" said I. "The *creatures* from Mars?"

"Quite enough I have," said the woman. "Thanks." And all three of them laughed.

I felt foolish and angry. "You'll hear more yet," I said, and went on to my home.

I startled my wife at the gate, so strange I seemed. I went into the dining room, sat down, drank some wine, and as soon as I could gather my wits I told her the things I had seen.

"They may come here," she said, putting her hand on mine.

"There is one thing," I said, trying to calm her fears, "they are the most sluggish things I ever saw crawl. They may keep the pit and kill people who come near them, but they cannot get out of it.—They can scarcely move."

I began to comfort her and myself by repeating all that Ogilvy had told me of the impossibility of the Martians establishing themselves on Earth. I laid stress on the problems of the difference in gravitational force here than on their planet. It is three times on Earth what it is on Mars. A Martian, therefore, would weigh three times more here, and his body would seem a covering of lead on him. This, indeed, was the general opinion, and both *The Times* and the *Daily Telegraph,* for instance, insisted on it the next morning in their pages, and both overlooked, just as I did, two obvious things.

The atmosphere of Earth, we now know, contains far more oxygen and far less argon than does Mars. The oxygen worked like magic on the strength of the Martians, and, in the second place, the Martians had such mechanical genius that they were almost able to do without the use of their bodies.

But I did not consider these points at the time, and I grew more courageous.

"Those Martians have done a foolish thing," I declared to my wife. "They have behaved in such fashion because, no doubt, they are terrified of us. Perhaps they expected to find no living things.—But now, if worst comes to worst, and they will not be peaceful, one bomb in their pit will kill them all."

This reasoning was probably similar to what the dodos on the island of Mauritius thought when a shipful of pitiless, hungry sailors landed on their shores: "We will peck them to death tomorrow."

In London that Friday night poor Henderson's telegram describing the gradual unscrewing of the capsule-lid was judged to be a hoax, and his evening newspaper, after telegramming him for verification and receiving no reply—the man was killed—decided not to print his story.

For the most part, daily life within even our five-mile radius of the catastrophe went on as usual. It was only round the edge of the common that any disturbance was noticeable. There were half a dozen villas burning on the Woking border. There were lights in all the houses on the common side of the three villages, and the people there kept awake till dawn.

That night nearly forty people lay under the starlight about the sandpit, charred and distorted beyond recognition, and all night long the common from Horsell to Maybury was deserted and brightly ablaze.

The news of the massacre probably reached Chobham, Woking, and Ottershaw at the same time. A number of people, attracted by the stories they had heard, were walking over the Horsell Bridge and along the road between the hedges that runs out at last upon the common.

A curious crowd lingered both on the Chobham and Horsell bridges. One or two adventurous souls, it was afterwards found, went into the darkness and crawled quite near the Martians, but they never returned, for now and again a heat-ray, like the beam of a warship's search-light, swept over the common and killed them. It is still a matter of wonder how the Martians are able to slay men so swiftly and so silently. Many think that in some way they are able to generate an intense heat in the ray-gun's special chamber. They project this intense heat in a beam against any object they choose, by means of a curved mirror of unknown material, much as the curved mirror of a lighthouse projects a beam of light. However it is done, it is certain that a beam of heat is the essence. Whatever is burnable flashes into flame at the touch of it: metal liquifies, water explodes into steam.

Charred bodies lay all about on the common all night under the stars, and all the next day. A noise of hammering from the pit was heard by many people.

So there you have the state of things on Friday night. In the center, sticking into the skin of our old planet Earth like a poisoned dart, was this cylinder. But the poison was scarcely working yet. Around it was a patch of silent common, smoldering in places, and a burning bush or tree here and there. Beyond was a fringe of excited, worried people, and beyond them, hardly any reaction at all. In the rest of the world the stream of life still flowed as it had flowed for thousands of years. The fever of war had not yet developed.

All night long the Martians were hammering and stirring, sleepless, at work upon machines. Every once in a while a puff of greenish-smoke whirled up to the starlit sky.

About eleven o'clock a company of soldiers came through Horsell, and arranged themselves along the edge of the common to form a human fence. Later a second company of soldiers marched through Chobham to fence off the north side. Several officers from the Inkerman barracks had been on the common earlier in the day, and one, Major Eden, was reported to be missing. The colonel of the regiment came to the Chobham bridge and was busy questioning the crowd at midnight. The military authorities were certainly alive to the seriousness of the business. About eleven, the next morning's papers were able to say that specially trained soldiers and four hundred men from the Cardigan regiment had set out for the area.

A few seconds after midnight the crowd in the Chertsey road near Woking saw a star fall from heaven into the pinewoods to the northwest. It had a greenish color, and caused a silent brightness like summer lightning. This was the second cylinder.

3. Mechanical Giants

SATURDAY LIVES in my memory as a day of suspense. It was hot. I had slept but little, and I rose early. I went into my garden before breakfast and stood listening, but towards the common there was nothing stirring but a lark. I also heard, from the station, a train running towards Woking.

The milkman came as usual. "They aren't to be killed," the milkman informed me, "if that can be avoided."

It was a most unexceptional morning. I saw my neighbor, Ross Robins, gardening and chatted with him for a time. He believed the troops would be able to capture or to destroy the Martians that day.

"It's a pity they make themselves so unapproachable," he said. "It would be curious to know how they live on another planet; we might learn a thing or two."

After breakfast, instead of working, I decided to walk down towards the common. Under the railway bridge I found a group of soldiers. They told me no one was allowed over the canal. I talked with these soldiers for a time. I told them of my sight of the Martians the previous evening. None of them had seen them, so they asked me many questions. I described the heat-ray to them, and they began to argue among themselves.

"Crawl up under cover and rush 'em, I say!" said one.

"Get out!" said another. "What's cover against this here heat? It's just sticks to cook you with! What we got to do is to go as near as the ground'll let us, and then drive a trench."

"Blow yer trenches! You always want trenches; you ought to've been born a rabbit, Snippy."

"Ain't they got necks, then?" said a third.

I repeated my description of them.

"Octopuses," said he, "that's what I calls 'em."

"It ain't no murder killing beasts like that," said the first speaker.

"Why not shell the darned things straight off and finish 'em?" said the third soldier. "You can't tell what they might do."

"Where's your shells, Jerv?" said the first speaker. "There ain't no time. Do it in a rush, that's my tip, and do it at once."

So they discussed it. After a while I left them, and went on to the railway station to get as many morning papers as I could. I did not get a glimpse of the common, for even the church towers were in the hands of the military authorities. The soldiers had made the people on the outskirts of Horsell lock up and leave their houses.

I got back to lunch about two, very tired, for, as I have said, the day was extremely hot and still. About half past four I went up to the railway station to get an evening paper, for the morning papers had contained only a very brief, and inaccurate, description of the killing of Stent, Henderson, Ogilvy, and the others. From the soldiers I gathered that the Martians did not show an inch of themselves. They seemed busy in their pit, and there was the sound of hammering and an almost continuous stream of smoke. Apparently they were getting ready for a fight.

All this preparation by both sides excited me. In my imagination I saw us defeating the invaders in dozens of ways. It hardly seemed a fair fight to me. They seemed helpless in that pit of theirs.

About three o'clock there began the thud of a gun from Chertsey. I learned that the pinewood into which the second cylinder had fallen was being shelled, in the hope of destroying that object before it opened. It was only about five o'clock, however, that a field gun reached Chobham for use against the first Martians.

About six in the evening as I sat at tea with my wife, I heard a muffled explosion from the common, and immediately after, a burst of firing. Soon after that came a rattling crash, quite close to us, that shook the ground, and, running outside, I saw the tops of the trees about the college burst into red flames, and the tower of the little church beside it slide down in a heap. One of our own chimneys cracked as if a shot had hit it, and a piece of it came clattering down the tiles and tumbled into the flower bed by my study window.

I and my wife stood amazed. Then I realized that the crest of Maybury Hill must be within range of the Martians' heat-ray now that the college was out of the way.

At that I gripped my wife's arm, and ran her out into the road. Then I fetched out our servant-woman.

"We can't possibly stay here," I told her and my wife. And as I spoke the firing began again on the common.

"But where are we to go?" said my wife in terror.

I remembered her cousins in Leatherhead. "Leatherhead!" I shouted above the noise.

She looked away from me downhill. The people were coming out of their houses.

"How are we to get to Leatherhead?" she said.

"Wait here," I said. "You are safe on this spot." And I started off at once for the pub, for I knew that the owner had a small horse-cart. I found him within the pub, unaware of what was going on behind his place.

I explained hastily that I had to leave my home, and needed to rent his cart. He agreed, surprised by my hurry, and I drove the horse and cart back to my home. I left it with my wife and our servant and ran into the house to load up our valuables. While I did this, the trees below the house were burning, and the fence up the road was glowing red. Soldiers were going from house to house, warning people to leave.

I asked him, "What's the news?"

"They're crawling out in a thing like a dish cover," he said, before running on. I jumped up on our cart, and away we went. In a few moments we were clear of the smoke and noise, and rushing down the opposite slope of Maybury Hill towards Old Woking.

Ahead was a quiet, sunny landscape, a wheat field on either side of the road. At the bottom of the hill we turned to look back at the hillside we were leaving. Thick streams of black smoke with threads of red fire were jetting up into the still air, and throwing dark shadows upon the green treetops eastward. The road was dotted with people running. And very faint now, one heard the whirr of a machine-gun and the cracking of rifle-shots.

Leatherhead is about twelve miles from Maybury Hill. We got there about nine o'clock, and the horse had an hour's rest while I took supper with my cousins and asked them to take care of my wife.

She was strangely silent throughout the drive, and seemed to believe there was nothing but doom ahead. I pointed out that the Martians were tied to the pit by their heaviness, and at the utmost could crawl a little out of it; but she was not reassured. She did not want me to return the cart to the pubkeeper, but to stay. I wish that I *had* stayed! But I could see no cause for robbing the pubkeeper of his transportation, should he need it as well.

I had been excited all day, struck with war-fever. I was not so very sorry that I had to return to Maybury that night. I wanted to see the end of the Martians.

It was nearly eleven before I started my return. The night was very dark, and it was as hot as the day. Fortunately, I knew the road well. As I rode through Ockham I saw along the western horizon a blood-red glow, which, as I drew nearer, crept slowly up the sky. The driving clouds of a gathering thunderstorm mingled there with masses of black and red smoke.

After midnight I came to a view of Maybury Hill, with its treetops and roofs black and sharp against the red. As I looked at it a weird green glare lit the road near me and showed the distant woods towards Addlestone. I saw that the driving clouds had been pierced by a thread of green fire, which descended into the field to my left. It was the third falling star!

Immediately after its crash-landing, lightning danced in the sky, and the thunder burst like a rocket overhead. My horse took the bit between his teeth and bolted. We clattered down the Maybury Hill as the lightning went on in quick flashes. The thunder seemed to crack from a machine.

I tried to pay attention to the road before me, but then I noticed something that was moving rapidly down the opposite slope of Maybury Hill. At first I took it for the wet roof of a house, but one lightning flash following another showed it to be rolling. I could not understand what I was seeing. A long stretch of lightning then showed me, in a flash that was as bright as daylight, this Thing!

How can I describe it? It was a three-footed mechanical monster, higher than the houses, striding over the young pine trees, and smashing them aside in its long paces. Its metal surface glittered; long steel ropes dangled from it, and it crashed along, each step like the thunder I had heard. Then the night was dark, and I waited for another flash of lightning, which came within seconds, and showed the monster leaning over one way with two feet in the air, and then, darkness, before the next flash showed the mechanical menace a hundred yards nearer.

Then suddenly the trees in the pinewood ahead of me were parted, as reeds are parted by a man thrusting through them; they were snapped off and driven down, as a second three-footed contraption came rushing towards me. And I was galloping hard to meet it! At the sight of the second monster my nerve went altogether. Not stopping to look again, I wrenched the horse's head hard round to the right, and in another moment the car had tipped over, and I was flung sideways and fell into a shallow pool of water.

I crawled out and crouched under a clump of bushes. The horse lay motionless, and by the lightning flashes I saw the colossal machine striding by me and passing uphill towards Pyrford.

Seen so close, the Thing was incredibly strange. Its long, flexible, glittering tentacles (one of which gripped a young pine tree) were swinging and rattling against the side of its body. The bronze hood on top of the body moved to and fro, like a head looking about. Behind the main body was a huge mass of white metal like a gigantic fisherman's basket, and puffs of green smoke squirted out from the joints of the limbs as the monster swept by me. And in an instant it was gone.

As it passed it put out a deafening howl of "Aloo! Aloo!" that drowned out the thunder. In another minute it was with its companion, half a mile away, stooping over something in the field. I have no doubt this Thing in the field was the third of the ten cylinders they had fired at us from Mars.

For some minutes I lay there in the rain and darkness watching, by the occasional flash of the lightning, these monstrous beings of metal moving about in the distance over the hedge tops. Now and then came a gap in the lightning, and the night swallowed them up.

I was soaked with rain from above and puddles below. It was some time before my astonishment would let me struggle up the bank to a drier position.

Not far from me was a little one-room hut of wood, surrounded by a patch of potato garden. I struggled to my feet at last, and, making use of every chance of cover, I made a run for this. I hammered at the door, but I could not make the people hear, and I turned away. I crawled along a nearby ditch, unobserved by these monstrous machines, into the pinewood towards Maybury.

Under cover of the wood I pushed on, wet and

shivering, towards my house. It was very dark in the wood, for the lightning was now becoming infrequent, and the rain was pouring down.

If I had fully realized the meaning of all the things I had seen I should have immediately gone back to rejoin my wife at Leatherhead. But that night things were so strange, and I was bruised, weary, wet, and deafened and blinded by the storm. I meant to go on to my own house. I staggered against trees, fell into a ditch, and finally splashed out into the lane that ran down from the College Arms. The storm water was sweeping the sand down the hill. There in the darkness a man blundered into me and sent me reeling back.

He gave a cry of terror, sprang sideways, and rushed on before I could gather my wits to speak to him. So heavy was the storm that I had to almost pull myself up the hill. I held onto a fence and worked my way along it. Near the top I stumbled upon something soft, and, by a flash of lightning, saw between my feet a man. He lay crumpled up close to the fence, as though he had been flung against it.

I overcame my horror and stooped and turned him over. I felt for his heartbeat, but it was gone. He was dead. Apparently his neck had been broken. The lightning flashed again and I sprang to my feet. I recognized the face as belonging to the landlord of the pub, the man whose cart I had taken.

I stepped over him and went on. Nothing was burning on the rainy hillside, though from the common there still came a red glare and smoke. I could see by the flashes the houses about me were mostly undamaged. Down the road towards Maybury Bridge there were voices and the sound of feet, but I had not the courage to shout or to go to them. I let myself in my house with my key, closed, locked, and bolted the door, staggered to the foot of the staircase, and sat down. My imagination was full of those striding metallic monsters, and of the dead body smashed against the fence.

I went upstairs to my study. The window there looks

over the trees towards Horsell Common. The thunderstorm had passed. The towers of the college and the pine trees that used to surround it were gone, and very far away, lit by a vivid red glare, the common's sandpits were visible. I saw huge black shapes, which moved busily to and fro.

It seemed as if the whole country in that direction was on fire—a broad hillside set with tongues of flame, swaying with the dying storm. Around the Woking station several of the houses and streets were glowing ruins. The light upon the railway puzzled me at first; from a black heap came a bright glare, and to the right of that a row of yellow boxes. Then I understood that this was a wrecked train, the front part smashed and on fire, and most of the cars still upon the rails.

At first I could see no people, but then later I saw against the light of Woking station a number of figures hurrying one after the other across the tracks.

This was the little world in which I had been living so safely and comfortably for years, this fiery chaos! I began to see that there must be some relationship between the mechanical giants and the sluggish lumps I had seen emerge from the cylinder. I sat and looked out the window at the blackened country, and particularly at the three gigantic black things that were going to and fro in the glare of the sandpits.

They seemed amazingly busy. I began to ask myself what could they be. Were they live machines? Such a thing I felt to be impossible. Or did a Martian sit within each, directing it, much as a man's brain sits and rules in his body? I began to compare the things to our machines, to ask myself how a train would seem to an animal.

The storm had left the sky clear, and over the smoke of the burning land the starlike pinpoint of Mars was dropping into the west, when I noticed a soldier coming into my garden.

I leaned out the window and whispered, "Psst!"

"Who's there?" he said, peering up.

"Where are you going?" I said.

"God knows!"

"Are you trying to hide?"

"Of course!"

"Come into the house," I said.

I went down, unfastened the door, and let him in.

"What has happened out there?" I asked.

"What hasn't?" he said. "They wiped us out—simply wiped us out." I gave him something to drink and he sat down at the dining table. He put his head on his arms and began to sob and weep like a little boy.

It was a long while before he could steady himself and answer my questions. He was a driver in the artillery, and had come into action at seven that night. Firing was going on across the common, and it was said that the first party of Martians were crawling slowly towards their second cylinder under the cover of a metal shield.

Later this shield staggered up on three legs and became the first of the three fighting-machines I had seen. The gun the soldier drove had come to a stop near Horsell, in order to fire upon the sandpits. But before they even had a chance to load up the gun, the fighting-machine fired a heat-ray and all the ammunition exploded. There was fire all about the soldier, and he found himself lying under a heap of charred men and horses.

"I lay still," he said, "scared out of my wits. We'd been wiped out like that! I had to lie there until I could worm myself out from beneath a horse. All of us—except for me—were wiped out!"

While under the horse he had peeped out at the common, where he watched soldiers from the other side make a rush at the sandpit. They were all killed by the heat-ray. Then the monster had risen to its feet, and had begun to walk leisurely to and fro across the common, with its headlike hood turning just like the head of a man under a cowl. A kind of arm held a metal case with a funnel, from which the heat-ray smoked.

In a few minutes there was, so far as the soldier could

see, not a living thing left upon the common, and every bush and tree upon it was burning. He heard guns from afar rattle for a time, and then become silent. The giant saved Woking station and its cluster of houses until the last; then, in a moment, the heat-ray came out and the town became piles of fiery ruins. Then the Thing shut off the heat-ray and, turning its back upon the soldier, began to waddle away towards the pinewoods that contained the second cylinder. As it did so a second glittering giant got up out of the sandpit.

The second monster followed the first, and so the soldier began to crawl across the hot heather ash towards Horsell. He managed to get into a ditch by the side of the road and so escaped to Woking. But he couldn't pass through there, as one of the Martian giants returned. He saw it chase a man, catch him with one of its steely tentacles, and knock the man's head against the trunk of a pine tree. At last, after nightfall, the soldier got over the railway embankment.

Since then he had been sneaking towards Maybury in the hope of getting out of danger. That was the story I got from him, bit by bit. He grew calmer telling me and trying to make me see the things he had seen.

When we had finished eating we went upstairs to my study, and looked again out of the window. In one night the green and pretty valley had become a valley of ashes. The fires had nearly gone out now, but there were many smoky streams. Dawn had come. Shining with the glow of the growing light of the east, three of the metal giants stood about the pit, their cowls rotating as though they were surveying the destruction.

It seemed to me the pit had been enlarged, and now and again puffs of green smoke streamed up and out of it.

4. One Dead Martian

AS THE DAWN grew brighter we went downstairs. The soldier agreed with me that the house was no place to stay. He wanted to rejoin his company, and I wanted to return at once to Leatherhead. I was determined to take my wife to Newhaven, and then out of the country. I knew that the area around London would be the scene of a terrible war before these creatures could be destroyed.

I thought we should start at once, but my friend knew we should pack all the food we could. Then we crept out of the house, and ran as quickly as we could down the road. The houses seemed deserted. In the road lay a group of three charred bodies close together, struck dead by the heat-ray. And here and there were things that people had dropped—a clock, a slipper, a silver spoon. At the corner was a little broken-wheeled cart, filled with boxes and furniture.

Except for the orphanage, which was on fire, none of the houses had suffered very much. The heat-ray had shaved the chimney tops and passed. Yet, except for ourselves, there did not seem to be a living soul on Maybury Hill. The majority of the citizens had escaped, I suppose, by way of the Old Woking road, or they had hidden.

We went down the lane, by the body of a man in black, and broke into the woods at the foot of the hill. We pushed through towards the railway without meeting a soul. There was not a breath of wind this morning, and everything was strangely still. Even the birds were hushed, and as we walked along the soldier and I talked in whispers and looked now and again over our shoulders.

After a time we drew near the road and saw three cavalry soldiers riding slowly towards Woking. We hailed them, and they halted while we ran towards them. It was a lieutenant and two privates.

"You are the first men I've seen coming this way this morning," said the lieutenant. "What's brewing?"

"Gun destroyed last night, sir," said my soldier friend. "I'm trying to rejoin my company. You'll come in sight of the Martians, I expect, about half a mile along this road."

"What the dickens are they like?" asked the lieutenant.

"Giants in armor, sir. Hundred feet high. Three legs and a body like 'luminum, sir, with a big, weird head in a hood, sir."

"What nonsense!" said the lieutenant.

"You'll see, sir. They carry a kind of gun, sir, that shoots fire and strikes you dead." The soldier began to describe the heat-ray.

"It's perfectly true," I said.

"Well," said the lieutenant, "I suppose it's my business to see it too. You'd better go and report to Brigadier-General Stephens, and tell him all you know. He's at Weybridge."

"Yes, sir."

"Half a mile, you said?" said the lieutenant.

"At the most!" I said, and pointed over the treetops southward. He thanked us and rode on, and we saw them no more.

By Byfleet station we came out of the pine trees and found the country calm and peaceful under the morning sunlight. We were far beyond the range of the heat-ray. Had it not been for the silence of the deserted houses and the soldiers standing on the bridges, it would have seemed like any other Sunday.

Through the gate of a field we saw, across a stretch of flat meadow, six big guns pointing towards Woking. The gunners stood by the guns waiting, and the ammunition wagons were close by.

"That's good," I said. "They will get one fair shot, anyway."

The soldier said, "It's bows and arrows against lightning! They haven't seen that Martian fire-beam yet."

Byfleet was turned upside down with people moving their possessions.

We saw one old fellow trying to lug a huge box containing flower pots. Soldiers were trying to convince him to leave it behind and he was angrily arguing with them.

I stopped and said to the old man, "Don't you know what's over there?" I pointed at the tops of the pine trees that hid the Martians.

"Eh?" he said, turning to me. "I was explaining to these blunderheads these orchids is valuable."

"Death!" I shouted. "Death is coming! Death!" I left him to try to comprehend that if he could, and hurried on after my companion. At the corner I looked back. The soldiers had left him, and he was still standing by his box, with the pots of orchids, and staring at the treetops.

I and the soldier went on and found a seat on the edge of a fountain to eat a meal with what we had brought with us. Patrols of soldiers, meanwhile, were warning people to move now or to take refuge in their cellars as soon as the firing began. A growing crowd of people had assembled at the railway station, and the swarming platform was piled with boxes and packages.

We remained at Weybridge until midday, and part of the time we spent helping two old women to pack a little cart. The river Wey has a triple mouth, and at this point boats are to be hired and there is a ferry across. As yet the flight of the townspeople had not become a panic, but there were already far more people than all the boats could carry.

There was a lot of shouting, but the idea people seemed to have was that the Martians were simply largish creatures who might attack the town, but would certainly be destroyed in the end.

Across the Thames, except just where the boats landed, everything was quiet, in contrast to the Surrey side. The people who landed there from the boats went tramping off down the lane.

Then the sound of guns came from the direction of Chertsey. The fighting was beginning. Almost immediately guns from closer by, near the pinewoods, started firing one after another. But nothing was to be seen by us at the river.

"The sojers'll stop 'em," said a woman beside me. A haziness rose over the treetops.

Then suddenly we saw a rush of smoke far away up the river. The ground quaked under us, and a heavy explosion shook the air, smashing two or three windows in the houses near.

"Here they are!" shouted a man. "Yonder! D'yer see them? Yonder!"

Quickly, one after the other, one, two, three, four of the armored Martians appeared, far away over the little trees, across the flat meadows that stretched towards Chertsey, and striding hurriedly towards the river. At first they seemed little cowled figures rolling along as fast as flying birds.

Then, advancing towards us, came a fifth. Their armored bodies glittered in the sun as they swept swiftly forward upon the guns, growing rapidly larger as they drew nearer. One on the extreme left flourished a huge gun high in the air, and the ghostly, terrible heat-ray I had already seen on Friday night struck the town.

At sight of these strange, swift, and terrible creatures the crowd near the water's edge was horror-struck. There was no screaming or shouting, but a silence. Then there was panic. A man swung round and struck me with his suitcase, and a woman pushed me as she rushed past. I thought about the heat-ray and shouted, "Get under the water! Everyone, under the water!"

But no one listened to me.

I rushed towards the approaching Martian, down to the gravelly beach, and headlong into the water. After all, others followed, but the water was so shallow that I ran perhaps twenty feet scarcely waist-deep. Then, as the Martian towered overhead a couple of hundred yards away, I flung myself forward under the surface. The splashes of the people in the boats leaping into the river sounded like thunderclaps in my ears.

But the Martian machine took no more notice of the people running this way and that than a man would of the confusion of ants in a nest against which his foot has kicked. When, half-drowned, I raised my head above water, the Martian's hood pointed at the guns that were still firing across the river, and as it advanced it pulled out the heat-ray.

In another moment it was on the bank, and in a stride had waded halfway across. The knees of its foremost legs bent at the farther bank, and in another moment it had raised itself to its full height again, close to the village of Shepperton. Immediately, the six guns which had been hidden behind the outskirts of that village fired. The explosions made my heart jump. The monster was already raising the heat-ray as the first shell from the guns burst six yards above its hood.

I gave a cry of surprise. I saw and thought nothing of the other four Martian monsters; my attention was upon this one. Two other shells burst in the air near the body as the hood twisted round and received the fourth shell clean in its face. The hood bulged, flashed, was whirled off in a dozen tattered fragments of red flesh and glittering metal.

"Hit!" I shouted.

I heard other exultant shouts from the people in the water around me.

The decapitated colossus staggered like a dizzy giant; but it did not fall over. The living Martian within the hood had been killed, and the Thing was now a mindless, whirling machine of destruction. It staggered along and

In another moment it was on the bank and had raised itself to its full height.

struck the tower of Shepperton Church, smashing it down, and blundered along, finally collapsing into the river out of my sight.

A violent explosion shook the air, and a spout of water, steam, mud, and shattered metal shot far up into the sky. As the heat-ray hit the water, the water hissed into steam, and in a moment a huge, scaldingly hot wave came sweeping up the river. We struggled towards the shore screaming and shouting. The fallen Martian came into sight downstream, lying across the river, and for the most part underwater.

Thick clouds of steam were pouring off the wreckage, and the gigantic limbs were churning the water and flinging a splash and spray of mud into the air. The tentacles swayed like living arms; and it was as if some wounded thing were struggling for its life amid the waves. Red-brown fluid was spurting out of the machine.

My attention was turned from this mechanical death by a sound like a siren. A man shouted to me and pointed. Looking back, I saw other Martians advancing with giant strides down the riverbank from the direction of Chertsey.

I quickly ducked under the water, and, holding my breath, stayed under the surface as long as I could. The water was growing hotter. When for a moment I raised my head to take breath and throw the hair and water from my eyes, the steam was rising in a whirling white fog. The noise was deafening. Then I saw the giants through the fog. They had passed by me, and two were stooping over the frothing ruins of their comrade.

The third and fourth stood beside him in the water, one perhaps two hundred yards from me, the other further on. The heat-rays were shooting their hissing beams this way and that.

The air was full of sound, a confusion of noise—the clanging din of the Martians, the crash of falling houses, the thud of trees, fences, sheds flashing into flame, and the crackling and roaring of fire. Dense black smoke was mingling with the steam from the river, and as the heat-ray shot out over Weybridge, flames erupted.

I stood there for a moment in the boiling water, feeling hopeless. I could see other people scrambling out of the water through the reeds, like little frogs hurrying through grass from an advancing man.

Then suddenly the white flashes of the heat-ray came leaping towards me. The houses caved in as they dissolved at its touch and darted out flames. The trees changed to fire. The ray flickered up and down the tow path, cutting down the people who ran this way and that. It swept along the river to Shepperton, and the water in its track rose in a boil. I hurried shoreward.

In another moment a huge boiling wave rushed upon me. I screamed aloud, and scalded, half-blinded, in agony, I staggered through the hissing water toward the shore. Had I stumbled and fallen, I would have been killed. Instead I threw myself, in full sight of the Martians, upon the broad, gravelly beach. I waited for death.

I have a hazy memory of the foot of a Martian coming down near my head, driving straight into the gravel, whirling its way this way and that, and lifting again; I seem to remember the four Martians carrying the debris of their comrade away. And then, very slowly, I realized that by a miracle I had escaped.

After learning of our puny power, the Martians retreated to their original position upon Horsell Common with their broken companion. Had they left their fallen comrade and pushed on, they would have destroyed the city at once, since there was nothing at that time between them and London.

But they were in no hurry. Every twenty-four hours another cylinder came. And meanwhile, our military and naval forces worked to build up their weaponry and positions. Every minute a fresh gun came into position until, before twilight, every hill and slope had a long-barrelled gun hidden upon it.

It would seem that the giants spent the earlier part of the afternoon in going to and fro, transferring everything from the second and third cylinders to their original pit. One of the giants stood guard over the pit while the other Martians got out of their machines and went down into the pit. They were hard at work there far into the night, and the towering pillar of green smoke that rose from there could be seen from dozens of miles away.

And while the Martians were preparing for their next venture and while England gathered its forces for battle, I made my way towards London.

I saw an abandoned boat drifting downstream. I swam after it and got in. There was no paddle, so I pushed along with my hands. I believed that the water gave me my best chance of escape should these giants return.

For a long time I drifted, and many of the houses facing

the river were on fire. I paddled with my nearly boiled hands and felt the sun scorching my back. Just past the bridge at Walton I could bear no more, and I landed on the Middlesex bank and lay down in the long grass. I suppose it was about four or five o'clock. I got up after a short while and walked perhaps half a mile without meeting a soul and so lay down again in the shadow of a hedge. I seem to remember talking to myself. I was very thirsty—the river water had been too hot to drink. I thought of my wife and despaired of ever finding her.

I fell asleep, and when I awoke, a curate from the local church was sitting beside me staring at the sky. It was sunset.

I sat up and said, "Have you any water?"

He shook his head. "You have been asking that for the last hour," he said. He must have found me a strange-seeming man—wearing soaking pants and socks, my face, chest, and shoulders blackened by smoke.

"What do these things mean?" he asked.

I stared at him and made no answer.

"What sins have we committed? After morning service, I was walking through the roads to clear my head, and then—fire, earthquake, death! What are these Martians?"

"What are we?" I answered.

He looked at me for some time and said, "What has Weybridge done? Everything gone—everything destroyed! Swept out of existence! Why?"

It was clear he had escaped from the destruction at Weybridge, and it seemed to me he had lost his mind in the event.

"Are we far from Sunbury?" I asked.

"What are we to do?" he said. "Are these creatures everywhere? Has the earth been given over to them?"

"Are we far from Sunbury?"

"Only this morning, there I was, leading the choir . . ."

"Things have changed," I said. "You must try to keep your head. There is still hope."

"Hope!"

"Yes." I began to explain my view, but his attention wandered, and he interrupted me.

"This must be the beginning of the end," he said. "The end! The great and terrible day of the Lord! When men shall call upon the mountains and the rocks to fall upon them and hide them—hide them from the face of Him that sitteth upon the throne!"

I got to my feet and laid my hand on his shoulder. "You are scared out of your wits, my friend."

"But how can we escape?" he asked suddenly. "They cannot be defeated."

"Yet one of them was killed back there three hours ago!"

"Killed!" he said. "How can God's agents be killed?"

"I saw it happen. And they are not sent by God! They are from Mars."

"Listen!" he said.

From beyond the low hills across the water came the dull thud of distant guns and a far-off weird crying. Then everything was still. High in the west a crescent moon hung above the smoke of Weybridge and Shepperton.

"We had better follow this path northward," I said.

5. In London

MY YOUNGER BROTHER was in London when the Martians came to Woking. He was a medical student, and he heard nothing of the arrival until Saturday morning. The newspapers explained, for example, that the Martians seemed incapable of moving from their pit due to the relative strength of the earth's gravity.

As a result of this misplaced confidence, there were no signs of unusual excitement in the streets of London. Nothing was known of the fighting on the night of my drive to Leatherhead and back.

My brother did not worry about me and my wife, as he knew from the description in the papers that the cylinder was a good two miles from my house. But he did make up his mind to come down on a train in order to see the Things before they were killed. When he arrived at the station, however, he learned there had been some accident that prevented trains from reaching Woking that night. No one in the London station connected the breakdown with the Martians.

About five o'clock that Sunday afternoon my brother returned to the station, and saw trains crammed with soldiers and cargo—guns and other weapons.

After dark he bought a special edition of a newspaper, and it was only then that he realized something of the full power and terror of these monsters. He learned that they were not merely a handful of small sluggish creatures, but they were in control of vast mechanical bodies; and they could move and destroy with such power that even the mightiest guns could not stand against them.

They were described as "vast spiderlike machines, nearly a hundred feet high, capable of the speed of an express train, and able to shoot out a beam of intense heat." Heavy losses of soldiers were mentioned, but the tone of the stories was optimistic: One of the Martians had been destroyed; so they were not invulnerable. They had retreated to their pit again. Guns were coming from all directions to stop them. No doubt the Martians were strange and terrible, but there could not be more than twenty of them against our millions. The public would be warned by the authorities in case of danger.

But my brother saw that people from Surrey were descending on London. He began to hope he would see me. One man, just off a bus, said, "I tell you, they're pots and kettles on stilts, striding along like men."

The pubs were full of fugitives from Surrey. The roads were full, but none of the people could give my brother any news of Woking except one man who assured him that Woking had been entirely destroyed the night before.

"I come from Byfleet," he said. "A man on a bicycle came through the place in the early morning, and ran from door to door warning us to get out. Then came soldiers. We went out to look, and there were clouds of smoke to the south—nothing but smoke, and not a soul coming from there. Then we heard the guns at Chertsey, and folks coming from Weybridge. So I've locked up my house and come on."

About eight o'clock in south London there was heard the noise of heavy firing. My brother walked and walked, looking for sign of me or more news of Woking. After midnight he noticed what seemed to be sheet lightning in the south. Finally he returned home and slept. About eight in the morning he woke to the sound of door knockers, feet running in the street, distant drumming, and a clamor of bells. He wondered whether the world had gone mad. Then he jumped out of his bed and ran to the window.

"They are coming!" bawled a policeman, hammering at a door. "The Martians are coming!"

My brother dressed at the window in order to miss nothing of the growing excitement in the street.

"London in danger of suffocation! Fearful massacres in the Thames Valley!" shouted newsboys.

London, which had gone to bed on Sunday night seemingly safe and sound, was awakened Monday morning to a vivid sense of danger.

Unable from the window to learn enough of the news, my brother went down and out into the street, just as the sky was turning pink with the early dawn. "Black smoke!" he heard people crying. My brother bought a newspaper and read: "The Martians are able to launch rockets filled with enormous clouds of black poison smoke. They have smothered our soldiers, destroyed Richmond, Kingston, and Wimbledon, and are advancing slowly towards London, destroying everything on the way. It is impossible to stop them. There is no safety from the Black Smoke but immediate escape."

The whole population of six million in the city of London would soon be running northward.

"Black smoke!" the voices cried.

The bells of the churches were clanging and overhead the dawn was growing brighter.

My brother returned to his room, put all his available money into his pockets, and went out again into the streets.

While my brother was watching the fugitives stream over Westminster Bridge and the curate was talking crazily to me, the Martians resumed their attack.

About eight o'clock three of them advanced from the pit and, advancing slowly and cautiously, made their way through Byfleet and Pyrford towards Ripley and Weybridge, and so came in sight of the guns. These three

Martians did not walk together, but in a line, each perhaps a mile and a half from his nearest fellow. They communicated with one another by means of sirenlike howls.

It was this howling and firing that the curate and I heard at Upper Halliford. The Ripley gunners, artillery volunteers, fired one wild, premature shot and then ran away on horse and foot through the deserted village while the Martian, without using his heat-ray, walked over their guns, and passed in front of them, and so came upon the guns in Painshill Park, which he destroyed.

The St. George's Hill men were hidden by a pinewood as they fired on the Martian nearest to them. The shells flashed all round him, and he was seen to advance a few paces, stagger and go down. Everybody yelled together, and the guns were reloaded in haste. The fallen Martian howled in his sirenlike way, and immediately a second giant, answering him, appeared over the trees to the south. A leg of the first Martian had been smashed by one of the shells. The whole second round of shells flew wide of the Martians, and immediately the second and newly-arrived third Martians shot their heat-rays at the battery. The ammunition blew up, the pine trees all about the guns flashed into fire, and only one or two of the men who were already running over the crest of the hill escaped.

The three Martians took counsel together, and the scouts who were watching reported that they remained without moving for the next half hour. The Martian who had been knocked down crawled slowly out of his hood. He was a small brown figure and apparently he worked on the repair of the leg. About nine he had finished, and within a few minutes the machine was upright and he was behind the cowl.

These three Martians then joined four other Martians, who had arrived each carrying a thick black tube. A similar tube was handed to each of the first three, and the seven Martians fanned out in a curved line and advanced.

A dozen rockets sprang out of the hills before them as soon as they began to move. At the same time four more machines, similarly armed with tubes, crossed the river and two of them came into sight of myself and the curate. The curate cried and began running, but I knew it was no good running from a Martian, and I turned aside and crawled through the dewy nettles and brambles into the broad ditch by the side of the road. He looked back, saw what I was doing, and turned to join me.

The occasional howling of the Martians ceased. They took up their positions in a twelve-mile crescent. They seemed in sole possession of the night, lit by the slender moon.

But facing that crescent of Martians the guns were waiting. The Martians had only to advance and instantly those guns would fire their shells. Did the Martians understand that we in our millions were organized, disciplined, working together? Or did they interpret our stinging shells as we would interpret the attack on us by a hive of bees?

Then, after a long time, came a sound like a distant gun. Another nearer, and then another. And then the Martian nearest us raised his tube and fired it. There was no flash when it landed, no smoke.

I clambered up the hedge to watch the result in Sunbury. As I did so another Martian fired his tube, and a projectile went hurtling towards Hounslow. But nothing seemed to happen on its impact.

The Martian began moving eastward along the riverbank.

Every moment I expected the fire of some hidden battery to spring upon him; but the evening calm was unbroken. The fire of the Martian grew smaller and finally he passed out of my sight. The curate and I went climbing after him. Towards Sunbury was a strange cone-like hill that had never been there before. And then, farther across the river, near Walton, we saw another such mysterious hill. But even as we watched, the hills began to flatten out.

I looked further north and there I saw another of these cloudy black hills.

We heard the Martians hooting to one another, and then the air quivered with the thud of their guns. But there was no response from our guns to theirs. Now at the time we could not understand these things, but later I learned the meaning of these mysterious smoke hills. Each of the Martians, standing in the great crescent formation, had discharged, by means of the gunlike tube he carried, a huge canister over whatever hill or cover for human artillery happened to be in front of him. Some fired only one of these, some two—as in the case of the one we had seen. These canisters smashed on striking the ground—they did not explode—and let out an enormous amount of heavy, inky vapor, which coiled and poured upward in a huge black cloud, a gassy hill that sank and spread itself slowly over the surrounding country. A mere whiff of that vapor was death to all that breathes.

This vapor was heavier than the densest smoke, so that it sank down through the air and poured over the ground in a liquid manner. And where it came upon water some chemical reaction occurred, and the surface would be instantly covered with a powdery scum that sank slowly. The vapor did not diffuse as a true gas would do. It finally hung together in banks and sank to the earth in the form of dust. The black smoke clung so closely to the ground that fifty feet in the air, on the roofs and upper stories of high houses and on big trees, there was a chance of escaping its poison.

One man who escaped told of the strangeness of the coiling flow, and how he looked down from the church spire and saw the houses of the village rising like ghosts out of its inkiness. For a day and a half he remained there, weary, starving, and sun-scorched.

So, setting about it as methodically as men might smoke out a wasps' nest, the Martians spread this strange poisonous vapor over the Londonward country. The horns of their crescent formation slowly moved apart. All night through they advanced. Never once, after the Martian at St. George's Hill was brought down, did they give the artillery the ghost of a chance against them. Wherever there was a possibility of unseen guns against them, a fresh canister of the black vapor was discharged, and where the guns were openly displayed the heat-ray was brought to bear.

Before dawn the black vapor was pouring through the streets of Richmond, and the population of London was being roused to escape.

So now you understand the roaring wave of fear that swept through London just as Monday was dawning. By ten o'clock all was confusion; the police and the railways had lost all organization.

All the railways headed north were being filled. People were fighting for standing room. The pressure of leaving led people away from the overcrowded railways to the northward running roads. By midday a Martian had been seen at Barnes, and a cloud of slowly sinking black vapor drove along the Thames and across the flats of Lambeth, cutting off all escape over the bridges.

My brother, after being unable to get aboard a North-Western train at Chalk Farm, was able to buy a bicycle. So he got out away from the fiercest panic, but a mile from Edgware the rim of his wheel broke, and the bike became unridable. He left it by the roadside and trudged through the village. He succeeded in buying some food at an inn before he proceeded towards Chelmsford, where he had friends. He followed a footpath eastward and passed several farmhouses. In a grassy lane near High Barnet, he happened upon two ladies who became his fellow travellers. He saved them from a couple of men who were trying to drag them out of the little pony-cart they had been driving. One of the ladies was simply screaming; the other, a dark, slender figure, slashed with her whip at the man who gripped her other arm.

My brother immediately shouted and hurried towards the struggle. Being an expert boxer, my brother knocked down the first man, and with his grip upon the second, who had been assaulting the lady, a third came from

The slender lady pulled out a revolver from her handbag and fired at the robbers.

nowhere and smashed him between the eyes. He stumbled and fell. He would have had little chance against the robbers had not the slender lady very pluckily pulled out a revolver from her handbag. She fired at the robbers about to attack my brother and missed. The robbers fled, and the lady gave my brother the gun.

The lady invited my brother to join her and her sister-in-law, so, quite unexpectedly, my brother found himself with a cut mouth, a bruised jaw, and blood-stained knuckles, driving along an unknown lane with these two women.

They had just come to Stanmore, where the slender woman's husband, a surgeon, had sent them on their way to Edgware, where he thought they would find a seat on a train. He had heard of the Martians' advance, and he wanted them to go on while he warned the neighbors. He would follow soon after, but there had been no sign of him.

That was the story they told my brother before they stopped again in New Barnet. He promised to stay with them until the husband to one, brother to the other arrived. They made a sort of camp by the wayside, and they fed the pony. He told them of his own escape from London, and all that he knew of these Martians and their ways. The sun crept higher in the sky. Several fugitives came along the lane, and my brother gathered such news as he could from them.

My brother thought it was hopeless to try to board the trains at St. Albans or New Barnet, as they would already be crowded with escaping Londoners. He suggested they set out across Essex towards Harwich and from there across the Channel to France.

They began to meet more people. My brother's party set out and went on before they found a crush of people in the road from London. My brother got out of the cart to lead the pony pace by pace down the lane.

"Make way! Push on!" cried various voices.

There were throngs of people on foot and an impassable tangle of carts and wagons. There was fear on everyone's faces. It was hot and dusty.

"Make way! The Martians are coming!" cried the voices.

To force their way into the flood of people, my brother plunged into the traffic on foot and held back a cart-horse while the slender lady drove the pony through. A wagon locked wheels for a moment and ripped a long splinter from the cart. In another moment they were caught and swept forward by the stream of people. My brother, with a cabman's whip-marks red across his face and hands, scrambled into the cart and took the reins.

"Point the revolver at the man behind us," he told her, "if he presses us too hard."

Then he began to look out for a chance of edging to the right across the road. But once in the stream there was almost no getting across. They were swept through with the flood of people and carts. They struck through Hadley, and there on either side of the road they came upon a great crowd drinking in the little river. And farther on, from a hill near East Barnet, they saw two trains running slowly one after another—swarming with people, with men even riding atop the coal behind the engines—going northward along the Great Northern Railway.

Near this place they halted for the rest of the afternoon, for they were utterly exhausted. They were hungry, and the evening became cold. At night many people came hurrying from the other direction and went off in the direction from which my brother had come.

On Monday the Martians could have killed the entire population of London, even as it scattered from the city. Seen from a hot-air balloon that June morning, one could have seen a gigantic stampede out of London. But destruction of all life did not seem their goal.

Southward the glittering Martians went to and fro, calmly and methodically spreading their poison clouds over this patch of country and that. They do not seem to have aimed at killing so much as squashing any fight in us humans. They exploded any ammunition they came upon, cut every telegraph wire, and wrecked railways here and there. They seemed in no hurry to extend their field and did not come beyond the central part of London all that day.

Until about midday the Thames was an astonishing scene. Steamboats and ships of all sorts lay there, tempted by the enormous amount of money fugitives were offering for passage away from London. But then, about one o'clock in the afternoon, a cloud of black vapor appeared between the arches of Blackfriars Bridge. At that the Thames became a scene of mad confusion, as boats and barges jammed in the northern arch of the Tower Bridge as they fled.

The sixth cylinder fell at Wimbledon (I will tell about the fifth cylinder in the next chapter). My brother, keeping watch beside the women in the cart in a meadow, saw the green flash of it far beyond the hills. On Tuesday his little group, still set upon getting across the sea, made its way through the swarming country towards Colchester. The news that the Martians were now in possession of the whole of London was confirmed. They had been seen at Highgate, but they did not come into my brother's view until the next day.

That was the day that the millions of London began to realize their need for food. As they grew hungry they began to steal from farmers, who responded by trying to defend their trees and animals. A number of people, like my brother, looked for their escape eastward rather than northward, while some desperate souls were even going back towards London to get food.

The Midland Railway Company had resumed their service. There were also posters announcing that large stores of bread would be distributed to the starving. But this news did not keep my brother from pressing eastward all day. That night the seventh cylinder fell on Primrose Hill in London.

On Wednesday the three fugitives—they had passed the night in a field of unripe wheat—reached Chelmsford, and there the citizens seized the pony as food. There were rumors of Martians at Epping. People were watching for Martians here from the church towers. My brother preferred to push on, in spite of the pony, in spite of their being hungry, and it was lucky he did. By midday they passed through Tillingham, which seemed to be deserted, but just beyond, at the sea, they came suddenly in sight of the most amazing crowd of boats and ships.

For after the sailors could no longer come up the Thames, they came on to the Essex coast, to Harwich and Walton and Clacton, and afterwards to Foulness and Shoebury, to pick up people. Close inshore were fishing boats, steam launches, yachts, electric boats; and beyond them ships of all sorts. But about a couple of miles out lay an ironclad, very low in the water, almost, to my brother's view, like a waterlogged ship. This was the *Thunder Child.* It was the only warship in sight, but far away to the right over the smooth surface of the sea lay a serpent of black smoke to mark the next ironclads of the Channel Fleet. They hovered in an extended line, steam up and ready for action.

At the sight of the sea, the slender lady, Mrs. Elphinstone, panicked. She had never been out of England before, and she seemed to imagine that the French might be as frightful as the Martians. Her wish was to return to Stanmore. They would find George, her husband, there.

It was with great difficulty that my brother and her sister-in-law were able to get her down to the beach, where soon my brother waved to some men in a paddle steamer. The sailors sent a rowboat to them, and my brother bought them passage. The steamer was going, these men said, to Ostend, Belgium.

It was about five o'clock in the afternoon when the steamer, dangerously crowded with passengers, set out. On board they could hear big guns going off in the south. The ironclad close by fired a gun and hoisted a string of flags to signal its comrades. A jet of smoke sprang out of her funnels.

Far away in the southeast the masts of the three ironclads rose one after another out of the sea, beneath clouds of black smoke. My brother saw a column of smoke on the coast. His little steamer was already flapping her way eastward, and the low Essex coast was growing hazy when a Martian appeared, small and faint in the distance, advancing along the muddy coast from the direction of Foulness. Everyone on board stared at the distant shape, higher than the trees or church towers, advancing with a leisurely stride.

It was the first Martian my brother had seen, and he was amazed watching this Titan wading farther and farther into the water. Then, far away, came another Martian, and then yet another, wading deeply through a shiny mud-flat. They were all stalking seaward, as if to intercept the escape of the numerous ships and boats. In spite of the full-speed ahead orders of the steamer's captain, it seemed that they were standing still in the water as the monster advanced.

Glancing northwestward, my brother saw the other ships trying to outrush each other from harm's way. Then, after a swift movement of the steamboat flung him headlong from the seat upon which he was standing, there was a shouting all about him. He sprang to his feet and saw to his right the *Thunder Child,* steaming along, coming to the rescue of the ships. The three Martians were so far out to sea that their legs were almost entirely underwater. The *Thunder Child* did not fire, but drove full speed towards them. The Martians seemed not to know what to make of this vessel. Perhaps they thought it was another being such as themselves. Had it fired one premature shell, they would have known what it was up to and have sent her to the bottom of the sea with a blast from the heat-ray.

Suddenly, however, the first Martian lowered his poison-gas tube and fired a canister at the ironclad. It hit her side and glanced off, and the ironclad pushed on, clear of the inky gas cloud. The Martians, for once, retreated, and began legging it towards the shore. But then one of them turned and fired the heat-ray. A bank of steam sprang from the water, as the ray passed through the iron of the ship's side like a white-hot iron through paper.

The next moment the heat-ray wielding Martian giant staggered and fell, water and steam shooting high in the air. The guns of the *Thunder Child* were going off one after the other. At the sight of this Martian being taken down by the *Thunder Child,* the passengers aboard my brother's steamer shouted "Hooray!"

The *Thunder Child,* though flames were shooting from its middle, was alive still, and her engines were working. It headed straight for the second Martian, which pulled out *its* heat-ray. The *Thunder Child* fired off its shots first,

Steam sprang from the water as the heat-ray passed through the ship's side.

and the Martian staggered and crumpled up like cardboard. My brother shouted with triumph, "Good shot, fellows!"

"That's two down, one to go!" called the steamer captain.

Everyone was cheering. But no one could see anything for the next several minutes on account of the steam that rose from the monstrous Martians. All this time, the steamer was paddling steadily out to sea and away from the fight. By the time the clouds cleared off, nothing could be seen of the *Thunder Child* or the third Martian, but the other ironclads were rushing towards the scene.

At last the coast grew too faint to see, and the steamer throbbed along to Belgium.

6. The Curate

I HAVE BEEN telling you of my brother's adventures, and now I return to my experiences with the curate. We were in the empty house at Halliford, where we had fled to escape the black smoke. We stayed there all Sunday night and all the next day—the day of the panic. We could do nothing except wait.

I could think of little but my wife. I thought of her at Leatherhead, terrified, in danger, mourning me as a dead man. I paced the rooms and cried aloud when I thought of how I was cut off from her. My only hope was to believe that the Martians were moving Londonward and away from her. As the curate only complained and muttered crazy, tearful words, I kept to myself as much as possible.

We had seen signs of people in the next house on Sunday evening—but I do not know who these people were nor what became of them. We saw nothing of them the next day. The Black Smoke drifted slowly all through Monday morning, creeping nearer and nearer, driving at last along the roadway outside the house that hid us.

A Martian came across the field at midday, cleaning up the black dust with a jet of superheated steam that hissed against the walls and smashed all the windows. When we looked out again, from our wet house, the country northward looked as though a black snowstorm had passed over it. Looking towards the river, we were astonished to see a weird redness mingling with the blackened meadows.

I understood that we were no longer hemmed in, that now we might get away. But the curate was frightened.

"We are safe here," he repeated, "safe—safe."

I got myself ready to leave him behind—would that I had! I looked for food and drink, and when it was clear to him that I really meant to go, with or without him, he suddenly roused himself to join me. We started about five o'clock along the blackened road to Sunbury.

In Sunbury, and along the road, were dead bodies, horses as well as men, overturned carts and luggage, all covered thickly with black dust. At Hampton Court we were relieved to find a patch of green that had escaped the poison clouds. We went through Bushey Park, with its deer going to and fro under the chestnut trees, and some men and women hurrying in the distance towards Hampton. These were the first people we saw that day.

And so we came to Twickenham. Away across the road the woods beyond Ham and Petersham were still on fire. Twickenham was undamaged by either heat-ray or black smoke, and there were more people about here, though none could give us news. For the most part they were like ourselves, taking advantage of a lull in the battle to shift their quarters. We crossed Richmond Bridge about half past eight. As we hurried across the bridge I noticed floating down the stream a number of large red blobby objects. I did not know what these were. On the Surrey side of the river was the black dust that had once been smoke; there were also bodies and more bodies. But we had no glimpse of the Martians until we were some way towards Barnes.

We saw in the blackened distance a group of three people running down a side street towards the river, but otherwise it seemed deserted. Up the hill Richmond was burning; outside the town of Richmond there was no trace of the black smoke. Then suddenly, as we approached Kew, a number of people came running, and the upper part of a Martian fighting-machine loomed in sight over the housetops, not a hundred yards from us. Had the

Martian looked down we would have perished. We were so terrified that we dared not go on, but turned aside and hid in a shed in a garden. There the curate crouched, weeping, and refused to move a muscle.

But my desire to reach Leatherhead would not let me rest, and in the twilight I ventured out again. I went through a bush, and along a passage beside a big house, and so came out upon the road towards Kew. I had left the curate in the shed, but he came hurrying after me.

That second start was the most foolhardy thing I ever did. For it was obvious the Martians were all around us. No sooner had the curate caught up to me than we saw either the fighting-machine we had seen before or another, far away across the meadows. Four or five people hurried away from it across the field, and the Martian was chasing them. In three strides he was among them, and they ran in all directions. He used no heat-ray to destroy them, but picked them up one by one. Apparently he tossed them into a big metal basket attached to his back. For what purpose was he collecting them alive?

We stood for a moment petrified, then turned and fled through a gate behind us in a walled garden, fell into a ditch, and lay there, scarcely daring to whisper. It was nearly eleven o'clock before we gathered courage to start again, sneaking along hedgerows and through farms. In one place we came upon a scorched and blackened area and a number of scattered dead bodies of men. The village of Sheen, however, had escaped destruction, but was silent and deserted. My companion suddenly complained of faintness and thirst, and we decided to enter one of the houses.

In the first house we entered I found nothing eatable left in the place but some moldy cheese. There was, however, water to drink; I also took a hatchet, which would help us break through any further doors.

We then crossed to another house. It was white, with a walled garden. In the pantry we found two loaves of bread in a pan, an uncooked steak, and half of a ham. There were nine bottles of beer under a shelf, and two bags of haricot beans and some limp lettuces. We found two bottles of wine, four cans of soup, three cans of salmon, and a tin of biscuits. I go into such detail because, as it happened, this would be our only food for the next two weeks.

We sat in the kitchen in the dark—for we dared not strike a light—and ate bread and ham. As we were eating there came from outside a blinding flash of green light. A moment later there was a terrible crash, and the house seemed to crumble down upon us. Glass came down, the plaster fell. I was knocked across the floor against the oven and stunned. I woke with the curate dabbing water over me.

"Are you better?" asked the curate in a whisper.

I sat up and nodded.

"But don't move," he said. "The floor is covered with smashed dishes. You can't possibly move without making a noise, and I believe *they* are outside."

We both sat quite silent, so that we could scarcely hear each other breathing. Everything seemed deadly still, but then some plaster slid down over us, and we heard outside, very near, a strange metallic rattle.

"What is it?" I asked.

"A Martian!" said the curate.

For a time I was inclined to think one of the fighting-machines had stumbled against our house. For the next three or four hours, until the dawn came, we scarcely moved. And then the light filtered in not through a window, which was black, but through a triangular opening between a beam and heap of broken bricks in the wall behind us. We now saw the kitchen more clearly.

The window had been burst in by the garden soil, which flowed over the table upon which we had been sitting and lay about our feet. Outside the soil was banked high against the house. At the top of the window frame we could see an uprooted drainpipe. The floor was littered with smashed dishes. The end of the kitchen towards the house was broken into, and since the daylight shone in

The window had been burst in by the garden soil and we could see an uprooted drainpipe.

there, it was evident that most of the house had collapsed. Contrasting with this ruin was a neat cupboard against the wall between the kitchen and the next room, the scullery. It was decorated with knickknacks, all of them upright and intact.

As the dawn grew clearer, we saw through the gap in the wall a Martian standing guard over a glowing cylinder. At the sight of the Martian we crawled as quietly as possible out of the kitchen and through a door to the scullery.

"The fifth cylinder," I whispered. "That explosion last night was the fifth shot from Mars. It has struck the house and buried us under the ruins."

"God have mercy upon us!" he said.

Outside there began a metallic hammering, then a loud hooting, and then a hissing of an engine. Soon a regular thudding made a vibration that made everything about us quiver. Then, for some reason, the light into the kitchen was blocked, and the ghostly kitchen doorway became absolutely dark. For many hours we must have crouched there, silent and shivering, until we fell asleep.

When I awoke I was very hungry. I told the curate I was going to seek food, and felt my way towards the pantry. He made no answer, but as soon as I began eating he came crawling after me.

After eating we crept back to the scullery, and there I must have dozed again. When I woke I was alone. The thudding vibration continued. I whispered for the curate several times, and then felt my way to the door of the kitchen. He was lying against the triangular hole that looked out upon the Martians.

I advanced, crouching and stepping with extreme care amid the broken crockery that littered the floor. I touched the curate's leg, and he kicked with such surprise that the vibration caused a piece of plaster to slide down with a bang. I grabbed his arm, fearing that he might cry out, and for a long time we crouched motionless. The falling plaster, however, gave us a new gap in the wall through which to look out onto what had been a quiet road.

The fifth cylinder must have fallen right into the middle of the house we had first visited. That building had vanished, completely smashed by the Martian rocket. The cylinder now lay deep in a hole, already vastly larger than the pit I had looked into at Woking. The ground all round it had splashed under that tremendous impact—"splashed" is the only word—and lay in heaped piles that hid the masses of nearby homes. Our house had collapsed backward; the front portion had been destroyed completely; by a chance the kitchen and scullery had escaped, and stood buried now under soil and ruins, closed in by tons of earth on every side except towards the cylinder. So there we were, hung on the very edge of the huge circular pit the Martians were making. The heavy beating sound was apparently just behind us, and every now and then a bright green vapor drove up like a veil across our peephole.

The cylinder was already opened in the center of the pit, and on the farther edge of the pit, amid the smashed and gravel-heaped shrubbery, one of the fighting-machines, deserted by its driver, stood stiff and tall against the evening sky. Strange creatures were crawling slowly and painfully near a strange, glittering, spider-like machine that was unpacking the cylinder. It had five tentacles about its body, and it was fishing out a number of rods, plates, and bars from the head of the cylinder. As it extracted them it deposited them upon a level surface of ground behind it. Its motion was so swift, complex, and perfect that at first it seemed alive.

I could see a Martian was operating it. Now I watched the other Martians crawling over the ground, and their gray-brown, shiny, leathery bodies were clearer to see. They had huge, round bodies—or, rather, heads—four feet in diameter, each body having in front of it a face. This face had no nostrils, but it had a pair of large, dark-colored eyes, and just beneath this a kind of fleshy beak. In the back of this head or body was a single drum-like surface—an ear. In a group round the mouth were sixteen slender, almost whiplike tentacles, arranged in two bunches of eight each. They seemed to be trying to raise themselves on these "hands," but, of course, with the increased weight from our denser gravity, this was impossible.

Their insides, as dissection by our scientists has since shown, were fairly simple. The greater part of the body was the brain, sending enormous nerves to the eyes, ear, and tentacles. Besides this were bulky lungs, into which the mouth opened, and the heart. But, for the most part, they were heads! They did not eat. Instead, they took the fresh, living blood of other creatures and *injected* it into their own veins. The idea of this is no doubt horribly repulsive to us, but at the same time I think that we should remember how repulsive our eating habits would seem to a rabbit.

In three other points their physiology differed strangely from ours. They did not sleep. They kept in action. In twenty-four hours they did twenty-four hours of work. In the next place, they did not produce children as we do. A young Martian was simply *budded* off his parent. The last important point in which their systems differed from ours was in what one might have thought an unimportant detail. Micro-organisms, which cause so much disease and pain on Earth, have either never appeared on Mars or they eliminated them years ago. Diseases never enter their way of life.

Speaking of the differences between life on Mars and Earth, I will talk here about the strange red weed they brought. Apparently the vegetable kingdom in Mars, instead of having green for its dominant color, is of a vivid blood-red tint. The seeds which the Martians brought with them gave rise in all cases to red-colored growths. The red creeper that came had a very short life, but in that time it grew quickly. It spread up the sides of the pit by the third or fourth day of our imprisonment, and its cactus-like branches formed a red fringe to the edges of our triangular window.

While I was still watching the Martians' sluggish motions in the sunlight and noting each strange detail, the curate pulled at my arm. I turned to his scowling face. He wanted the window, which permitted only one of us at a time to peep through; and so I gave it up to him.

When I had my turn again, the busy crab-like machine had already put together several of the pieces it had taken out of the cylinder and formed them into a shape like its own. Down on the left a digging machine had come into view; it shot off jets of green vapor and worked its way round the pit, digging and moving the dirt. It piped and whistled as it worked. So far as I could see, the thing was without a Martian directing it at all.

The arrival of a second fighting-machine drove us from our peephole into the scullery, for we feared that from his height the Martian might see down upon us behind our barrier. Yet terrible as was the danger, the attraction of peeping was for us irresistible. In spite of the danger we would race across the kitchen in silence and push each other away from the hole.

When in the scullery the curate would sometimes weep for hours. To comfort himself he was eating too much, and it was in vain that I pointed out to him that our only chance of survival was to stay in the house until the Martians were through with their pit. We would need to conserve our food and drink.

As the days wore on I began to hate the curate. It is disagreeable to write these things, but I set them down so that my story may lack nothing.

Back at the peephole we discovered that three fighting-machines had come to the pit. The last two had brought with them new machines that stood in an orderly manner about the cylinder. The second handling-machine was now completed, and it was digging out and flinging masses of clay into a sort of smelting machine. It made, in a matter of minutes, bars of aluminum. Between sunset and starlight this machine must have made more than a hundred bars out of the crude clay.

The curate had possession of our slit when the first men were brought to the pit. I was sitting below, huddled up, listening. He made a sudden movement backward, and I, fearful that we had been seen, crouched in terror. He came sliding down the rubbish and crept beside me in the darkness unable to speak, but pointing and pointing at the hole. I stepped across him and clambered up to it. At first I could see no reason for his frantic behavior. The twilight had now come, the stars were faint, but the pit was lit by the flickering green fire that came from the aluminum-making. Then, amid the clangor of the machinery, came the odd sound of human voices.

I crouched, watching one of the fighting-machines, which stood across the pit. Its hood opened and there sat a bright-eyed, oily-skinned Martian. Suddenly I heard a yell and saw a long tentacle reaching over the shoulder of

Then a man, struggling, was lifted high.

the machine to the little cage that hunched upon its back. Then a man, struggling, was lifted high. In another moment I lost sight of him, and then began a shrieking and a long and cheerful hooting from the Martians. What horror was going on? They were consuming him, injecting his blood into theirs!

It was the only occasion on which I actually saw the Martians feed. After that experience I avoided the hole in the wall for the better part of a day. I went into the scullery and spent some hours digging with my hatchet as silently as possible; but when I had made a hole about a couple of feet deep the loose dirt collapsed noisily, and I did not dare continue.

On the fourth or fifth night I heard a sound like heavy guns. I was surprised to learn by this that we were still fighting the Martians.

It was on the sixth day of our imprisonment that I peeped out for the last time. The curate had stayed in the scullery. After some time I went back to see what he was doing. In the darkness I snatched from his lips our last bottle of wine.

We wrestled each other for it, and then the bottle fell and broke. I pulled away, but then planted myself between him and the food, and told him of my determination to begin a budget for our eatables. I divided the food in the pantry into rations to last us ten days. I would not let him eat any more that day. In the afternoon he made a feeble attempt to get at the biscuits, and I fought him off.

And so our uneasy companionship became a battle. For two long days we fought in whispers and wrestling contests. He was beyond reason. He would not stop in his attempts to get at my share of the food; he would not stop his noisy babbling to himself. I began to understand that he had gone completely insane.

On the eighth day he began to talk aloud instead of whispering, and nothing I could do would quiet him. "The word of the Lord is upon me!" he shouted. "I must go and call my brothers to repent!"

He rushed out of the scullery, and I rushed after him into the kitchen. "Repent!" he cried out. I picked up a brick and knocked him over the head. He fell on the floor, and I stood over him, panting. He was out cold.

Suddenly I heard a noise from outside. There was the sound of slipping and smashing plaster, and the triangular hole in the wall suddenly darkened. I looked up and saw one of the handling-machines at the hole. One of its gripping limbs curled slowly through the debris; then another limb appeared, feeling its way over the fallen beams. I stood petrified, staring. Then I saw through a sort of window near the edge of the machine the face and large dark eyes of a Martian, peering in, and then a long metallic snake of tentacle come feeling through the hole.

I turned, stumbling over the curate, and stopped at the scullery door. The tentacle was now two yards into the room, and twisting and turning with odd sudden movements this way and that. Then I fell into the scullery, trembling. I crept into the coal cellar and stood there in the darkness staring at the faintly lit doorway into the kitchen and listening.

Something was moving to and fro in the kitchen, very quietly. Every now and then it tapped against the wall, or started on its movements with a faint metallic ringing. Then a heavy object—I knew too well what it was—was dragged across the floor of the kitchen towards the opening. I crept to the door and peeped into the kitchen. In the triangle of bright outer sunlight I saw the Martian, in its handling-machine, studying the curate's head. I thought from the mark of the blow on the curate's head it would figure out that there was another human within.

I crept back to the coal cellar, shut the lid, and began to cover myself up as much as I could and as noiselessly as possible in the darkness, among the firewood and coal. After several minutes I heard the faint metallic jingle return. I traced it slowly feeling over the kitchen. Soon I heard it nearer—in the scullery. I thought that it might not be long enough to reach me. It passed, scraping faintly across the cellar door. Then I heard it fumbling at the latch! It had found the door! The Martians understood doors!

It played at the latch for minute, and then the door opened.

In the darkness I could just see the thing—like an

*I could see the thing—like an elephant's trunk—
waving towards me.*

elephant's trunk more than anything else—waving towards me and touching and examining the walls, coal, wood, and ceiling. Once, even, it touched the heel of my boot. I was on the verge of screaming. For a time the tentacle was silent. I thought perhaps it had withdrawn, but then, suddenly, with a click, it grabbed something—I thought it had me!—and seemed to pull out of the cellar again. For a minute I was not sure. Apparently it had taken a lump of coal to examine.

Then I heard the slow sound creeping towards me again. Slowly, slowly it drew near, scratching against the walls and tapping the furniture.

It bounced against the cellar door and closed it. I heard it go into the pantry, and the biscuit-tins rattled and a bottle smashed, and then came a heavy bump against the cellar door. Then there was silence.

Had it gone? At last I decided that it had. It came into

the scullery no more; but I lay all the tenth day in the cramped, stuffy darkness, buried among coal and firewood, not daring even to crawl out for a drink for which I craved. It was the eleventh day before I ventured from the coal cellar. The first thing I did before I went into the pantry was to fasten the door between the kitchen and the scullery. But the pantry was empty; every scrap of food was gone. Apparently, the Martian had taken it all on the previous day. So on this and the next day, I had nothing to drink or eat.

All I could think about was eating. I thought I had become deaf, for the noises I was expecting to hear from the pit had disappeared. I did not feel strong enough to crawl noiselessly to the peephole, or I would have gone there to see for myself.

On the twelfth day my throat was so parched that, taking the chance of making noise, I used the creaking rainwater pump that stood by the sink and got a couple of glassfuls of blackened water. I felt bolder once I saw that no tentacle came searching for me through the peephole.

On the thirteenth day I drank some more water, and dozed and thought of eating and escaping. The light that came into the scullery was no longer gray, but red. On the fourteenth day I went into the kitchen, and I was surprised to find that the fronds of the red weed had grown right across the hole in the wall. It was early on the fifteenth day that I heard a weird, familiar sound from near the kitchen—the snuffing and scratching of a dog! Going into the kitchen I saw a dog's nose peering in through a break in the red fronds. At the scent of me he barked shortly.

I crept forward, saying, "Good dog!" But he withdrew his head and disappeared. I listened and certainly the pit was still. I heard a sound like the flutter of a bird's wings and a hoarse croaking.

For a long while I lay close to the peephole, but not

daring to move aside the red plants that blocked it. Once or twice I heard a faint pitter-patter like the feet of the dog going here and there, and there were more birdlike sounds. At length I looked out.

Except in the corner, where crows hopped and fought over the skeletons of the men the Martians had eaten, there was not a living thing in the pit. I stared about me, scarcely believing my eyes. All the machinery was gone. I thrust myself out through the red weed and stood upon a mound of rubble. I could gaze in any direction except behind me, to the north, and there were no Martians to be seen. My chance of escape had come. With my heart throbbing, I scrambled to the top of the mound in which I had been buried for so long.

I looked about again, to the north as well, but no Martian was visible.

The day seemed dazzlingly bright, the sky a glowing blue. A gentle breeze kept the red weed gently swaying. And oh! the sweetness of the air! I had expected to see Sheen in ruins—indeed, I found about me the landscape of another planet. When I had last seen this part of the town in the daylight it had been a nice street of comfortable houses with shady trees. Now I stood on a mound of smashed brick, clay and gravel, over which spread hundreds of red cactus-like plants, knee-high. The trees near me were dead and brown. The neighboring houses had all been wrecked, but none had been burned; their walls stood, sometimes to the second story, with smashed windows and shattered doors. The red weed grew in the roofless rooms. Below me was the pit, with the crows fighting for food. A number of other birds hopped about among the ruins. Far away I saw a skinny cat slink along a wall, but there were no signs of humans.

I felt as a rabbit might feel returning to his burrow and suddenly seeing a dozen busy construction workers digging the foundations of a house where his home had been. I felt dethroned, that I was no longer a master, but an animal among the animals, under the Martian rule. With us it would be as with animals, to lurk and watch, to run and hide.

But so soon as I thought this I was back to thinking of my hunger. I saw, beyond a red-covered wall, a patch of garden. Here I found some young onions and carrots, all of which I gathered up, and, scrambling over a ruined wall, went on my way through red trees towards Kew. Some way farther, in a grassy place, was a group of mushrooms, which I devoured.

At Putney the bridge was almost lost in a tangle of the red weed. In the end, of course, the red weed died almost as quickly as it had spread. A bacterial infection soon seized it. All of our plants have acquired the resistance to bacterial diseases—they never fall to it without some struggle, but the red weed rotted like a thing already dead. The fronds became bleached, and then shriveled up and became brittle. They broke off at the least touch, and the waters that spurred their early growth carried their dried carcasses out to sea.

By the time I reached Putney Common the red weed had become sparse. The tall trees were free of the red creeper. There were wrecked houses but also perfectly preserved houses. I searched the secure houses for food, but they had already been ransacked. I spent the day resting in the cover of a bush. All this time I saw no human beings, and no signs of Martians. After sunset I struggled on along the road towards Putney, where I think the heat-ray was used. And in a garden beyond Roehampton I found young potatoes. From the garden all I could see were blackened trees, ruins, and down the hill the river, tinged with red weed.

For a time I believed that mankind had been swept out of existence, and that I stood there alone, the last man left alive. The Martians, I thought, had gone on and left the country, seeking food elsewhere. Perhaps even now they were destroying Berlin or Paris.

7. The War Is Over

I SPENT THAT night in an inn that stands on the top of Putney Hill. I found biscuits and two tins of pineapple. My mind became clearer, and I thought of my wife, and I was filled with worry.

In the morning I set out on the road to Wimbledon. I had an idea of going to Leatherhead, though I knew that I had little chance of finding her. When I reached the Wimbledon Common I came upon a busy swarm of little frogs in a swampy place among the trees. I stopped to look at them noisily croaking, and noticed something crouching amid a clump of bushes. A man rose up with a sword.

"Where do you come from?" he said.

"From Mortlake. I was buried near the pit the Martians made about their cylinder. I have worked my way out and escaped."

"There is no food here," he said. "This is my country. All this hill down to the river, and back to Clapham, and up to the edge of the common. There is only food for one. Which way are you going?"

"I think I shall go to Leatherhead."

Suddenly he pointed at me. "You! You're the man from Woking!"

"You are the artilleryman who came into my garden!"

He laughed and offered his hand. "I got away, don't you know. But look, it's not sixteen days since, and your hair's gone gray."

"It's no wonder.—But have you seen any Martians?" I asked.

"They've gone away across London," he said. "I guess they've got a bigger camp there. At night, all over there, the sky is alive with their lights. You can just see them moving. But nearer, I haven't seen them for five days. I do believe, though, that they've built a flying-machine."

"It is all over for us, then," I said. "If they can do that they will simply go round the world destroying mankind."

"They will—but at least it will relieve things over here a while. Anyway, it already is all over. Of all their giants, they've lost one—just one! They've walked over the body of England. The death of that one in Weybridge was an accident. And these are only the Martians' *pioneers*! We're beat, man!"

I made no answer.

"This isn't a war," said the soldier. "It never was a war, any more than there's a war between man and ants.—Only, of course, to them we're eatable ants."

"But if that is so, what is there to live for?"

"Men like me are going to go on living—for the sake of the breed. I tell you, I'm grim set on living. But we've got to learn before we've got a chance."

"What are you doing?" I asked. "What plans have you made?"

"Well, it's like this. We have to invent a sort of life where men can live and breed, and be safe enough to bring the children up. You see, how I mean to live is underground. Under this London are miles and miles of drains. A few days' rain will leave them sweet and clean. And the railway tunnels and subways, eh? Our new home! And so we form a gang of strong, good men and women. We can't have the weak or silly. We must keep up mankind's science and learning. That's where men like you might come in. We must learn more. We must watch these Martians. What if we learn how to shoot their heat-rays and operate those fighting-machines? We could fight 'em on their own terms. Think of it! We steal or make some of their weapons, and we surprise 'em! 'Hoot, hoot!' they say. 'Toodle-oo!' we say, and *swish,* out comes our heat-ray, and, just like that, mankind has come back to power!"

He talked in this fantastic manner through the morning, and we later crept out of the bushes, and, after scanning the sky for Martians, hurried to the house on Putney Hill where he had made his lair.

We went together to the roof and stood on a ladder peeping out of the roof door. No Martians were to be seen, so we ventured out and sat down. We could see the river, a bubbly mass of red weed, and low parts of Lambeth. Beyond Kensington dense smoke was rising, and that and a blue haze hid the northward hills.

That night, under the influence of his confident talk, and after a good, big meal, we drank champagne, smoked cigars, and played cards. At some point it came to me that such behavior in the face of mankind's destruction seemed madness. That very minute I resolved to leave this strange dreamer and go on to London and from there to Leatherhead and my wife.

In the morning I went down the hill, and by the High Street across the bridge to Fulham. The red weed nearly choked the bridge roadway, but its fronds were already whitened in patches by the spreading disease that soon killed it.

There was black dust along the roadway from the bridge onwards, and it grew thicker in Fulham. The streets were horribly quiet. I got food—sour, hard, and moldy rolls, but quite edible—in a bakery here. Some way towards Walham Green the streets became clear of powder. Going on towards Brompton I came upon the black powder in the streets and many dead bodies. They had been dead many days, and I hurried quickly past them.

Where there was no black powder, it was like a Sunday in the City, with the closed shops, the houses locked up, and the blinds drawn. The farther I went into London the more still it became. In South Kensington the streets were clear of dead and of black powder. It was near here that I first heard the howling. It sobbed: "Ulla, ulla, ulla, ulla." I went on towards the iron gates of Hyde Park. "Ulla, ulla, ulla," it wailed. I went on up the Exhibition Road. Near the park gate I came upon a strange sight—an overturned bus and the skeleton of a horse picked clean. Then I went on to the bridge over the Serpentine. The howling voice grew stronger and stronger, though I could see nothing above the housetops on the north side, except a haze of smoke to the northwest.

"Ulla, ulla, ulla, ulla!" cried the voice from the district about Regent's Park. I came into Oxford Street by the Marble Arch, and here again were the black powder and several bodies, and an evil smell from the gratings of the cellars of some of the houses. With great trouble I managed to break into a pub and get food and drink. I was weary after eating, and I went into the parlor behind the bar and slept on a sofa.

I awoke to find the dismal howling still in my ears, "Ulla, ulla, ulla, ulla, ulla." It was now dusk, and after I had found some biscuits and cheese, I wandered on to Baker Street. As I emerged from the top of Baker Street, I saw far away over the trees in the clearness of the sunset the hood of the Martian giant from which this howling proceeded. I watched him for some time, but he did not move.

I turned back away from the park and into Park Road, intending to go around the park, go along and get a view from St. John's Wood of this howling Martian. A couple of hundred yards along I heard a yelping chorus, and saw a dog with a piece of red meat in his jaws coming towards me and then a pack of starving dogs chasing him. As the yelping died away down the silent road, the wailing sound of "Ulla, ulla, ulla, ulla," came back into my hearing.

I then happened upon a wrecked handling-machine halfway to St. John's Wood station. At first I thought a house had fallen across the road. It was only as I clambered among the ruins that I saw this mechanical Samson lying, with its tentacles smashed and twisted, among the ruins it had made. The twilight was now so far advanced that I could see neither the blood with which its operating chair was smeared nor the gnawed body of the Martian that the dogs had found.

I pushed on towards Primrose Hill. Far away, through a gap in the trees, I saw a second Martian, as motionless as the first, standing in the park near the zoo. As I crossed the bridge the sound of "Ulla, ulla, ulla, ulla," suddenly switched off.

Night was coming, and all was terribly silent. I was terrified. In front of me the road became black. I ran off towards Kilburn and I hid in a cabmen's shelter in Harrow Road. But before dawn my courage returned, and while the stars were still in the sky I headed towards Regent's Park. In the half-light of early dawn, I came to the curve of Primrose Hill. On the summit, towering up to the fading stars, was a third Martian, motionless like the others.

I marched on recklessly towards this Titan, and then, as I drew nearer and the light grew, I saw that dozens of black birds were circling and clustering about the hood. At that sight my heart gave a bound of hope, and I began running along the road.

I came to the great mounds that had been heaped about the top of the hill—beyond was the final and largest pit the Martians had made—and from behind these heaps there rose a thin smoke against the sky. Against the skyline a dog ran. I felt no fear, only a wild excitement as I hurried up the hill towards the motionless monster. Out of the hood hung long shreds of brown flesh, at which the hungry birds pecked and tore.

In another moment I had scrambled up the mounds, and the pit was below me. There were gigantic machines here and there and huge piles of building material. And scattered around, some in their overturned war-machines, some in the now stiff handling-machines, and a dozen of them stark and silent and laid in a row, were the Martians—*dead!*—killed by the bacteria against which their systems were unprepared; killed as the red weed was killed; killed, after all man's weapons had failed, by the humblest things that God, in his wisdom, has put upon this Earth.

These germs have taken their toll of humanity since the beginning of time, but by virtue of natural selection have developed resistance. There are no bacteria on Mars, and as soon as these invaders arrived, as soon as they drank and ate, our microscopic allies began to work their overthrow. Even when I was watching them destroy the countryside and Weybridge, the Martians were doomed, dying and rotting as they went to and fro.

I stood staring into the pit, and my heart felt light. These things that had been alive and so terrible to men were dead. A pack of dogs, I could hear, fought over the bodies that lay darkly in the depth of the pit, far below me. Across the pit on its farther lip, flat and vast and strange, lay the great flying-machine that they had been experimenting on when decay and death stopped them. Death had come not a day too soon.

I turned and looked down the slope of the hill to where, circled now by birds, stood those other two Martians that I had seen overnight, just as death had overtaken them. The one had died, even as it had been crying to its companions. They glittered now, harmless tripod towers of shining metal, in the brightness of the rising sun.

The war was over. Even that day the healing would begin. Survivors would begin to return to London from across England and Europe. The pulse of life would beat again in the empty streets and pour across the vacant squares.

And now comes the strangest thing in my story. I remember all I did that day until the time that I stood weeping and praising God upon the summit of Primrose Hill. And then I forget.

Of the next three days I know nothing. I have learned since that, so far from my being the first discoverer of the Martian overthrow, several such wanderers as myself had already discovered the invaders' end the previous night. One man—the first—had managed to telegraph to Paris. From there the joyful news had flashed all over the world. The same day, men and women were hurrying to London, and food was pouring into our country from our relieved brothers in Europe. But of all this I have no memory. I drifted—a crazed man. When I came to, I found myself in a house of kindly people, who had found me on the third day wandering, weeping, and raving about my wife in Leatherhead.

Very gently, when my wits and health returned to me, they told me what they had learned of the fate of Leatherhead. Two days after I was imprisoned it had been destroyed, with every soul in it, by a Martian.

I was a lonely man, and they were very kind to me. I remained with them for four days. All that time I felt a craving to look once more on my old home, whatever there was that remained of it. And so I set out, through a busy London, and made my way to the little house at Woking. I took a train and looked at the ruins of the country. I got off at Byfleet station and took the road to Maybury, past the place where I and the artilleryman had talked to the soldiers, and on by the spot where the Martian had appeared to me in the thunderstorm. I turned off the road to find, among a tangle of red weeds, the broken cart I had ridden. Next to it were the bones of the horse.

Then I returned through the pinewood, and so came home past the College Arms. A man standing at an open cottage door greeted me by name as I passed.

I looked at my house with a quick flash of hope. The curtains of my study fluttered out of the open window from which I and the artilleryman had watched the dawn. No one had closed it since. I stumbled into the hall and the unlocked house felt empty. I saw the muddy footsteps I and the soldier had made going up the stairs.

I followed them to my study, and found lying on my writing-table the sheet of work I had left on the afternoon

I turned, and there were my cousin and my wife.

of the opening of the cylinder. I went downstairs and into the dining room. And then a strange thing occurred.

"It is no use!" said a voice. "The house is deserted. No one has been here. Do not stay here to torture yourself. He did not escape."

I was startled. I turned, and the glassed door was open behind me. I made a step to it and stood looking out.

And there, amazed and afraid, were my cousin and my wife. My wife gave a cry.

"I came home," she said, "because I knew—I knew—"

She swayed, nearly fainting, and I made a step forward and caught her in my arms.